Only an hour before, Hannah had been feeling pretty sorry for herself. Now she felt almost giddy with relief. There was obviously no real connection between Rachel and Dylan. "So... you guys never got to Part Two of the evening?"

"Oh, yeah, we did," Rachel replied. "I finally threw myself at him, just to shut him up."

Hannah's heart sank. "You kissed him?"

"Of course. Dylan's a totally great kisser," Rachel confided. "He's got very soft lips."

Hannah didn't want to hear any more...

Read more

Love Letters ♥

Perfect Strangers

Mixed Messages

Love Letters:
the write stuff

JAHNNa N. MALCoLm

SIMON AND SCHUSTER

SIMON AND SCHUSTER
First published in Great Britain in 2006 by Simon & Schuster UK Ltd
Africa House, 64-78 Kingsway, London WC2B 6AH
A Viacom company.

Originally published in 2005 by Simon Pulse,
an imprint of Simon & Schuster Children's Division, New York.

Text copyright © 2005 by Jahnna Beecham and Malcolm Hillgartner
Cover illustration © 2005 Jerry Paris
Cover design by Tracey Hurst

A CIP catalogue record for this book is available from the British Library.

This book is a work of fiction. Names, characters, places and incidents are either
products of the author's imagination or are used fictitiously. Any resemblance to actual
events or locales or persons, living or dead, is entirely coincidental.

ISBN: 1-416 -91073-5
EAN: 9781416910732

1 3 5 7 9 10 8 6 4 2

Printed and bound in Great Britain by Bookmarque Ltd, Croydon, Surrey

1

"Pardon me."

"Hmm?" Hannah Briggs raised her head. She had been studying her day planner in her locker, completely oblivious to the mob of students swarming around her in the hall.

"I'm a bit lost," the voice continued.

Hannah turned to see who was talking and bumped into the chest of a boy standing right behind her.

"Oh!" she gasped, stumbling backward.

"Hold on!" He reached out and caught her by the waist before she could fall back into her open locker.

Hannah grabbed his arm to steady herself. When she finally looked up into the boy's face, she nearly collapsed again. There was no doubt about it. The most handsome boy ever to tread the halls of Red Rocks High was standing at her locker, his arms wrapped around her waist.

For a second Hannah wondered if she was having some sort of weird hallucination. She'd spent the night before watching *American Idol* and flipping through *Teen People* magazine at her friend Rachel's house. Staring at all of those Hollywood hunks could have done something to her brain. Just to make sure he was no illusion, Hannah squeezed the boy's arm. He was real, all right.

"I don't know whether to let go of you and back away, mortified," the boy confessed, "or continue holding on. It's quite nice, actually."

Hannah just stood there, staring up into his dark green eyes. They were rimmed with long, dark lashes.

"You're British," she managed to choke out at last.

"Why, yes, I am." The boy grinned, revealing a tiny dimple at the corner of his mouth. "What gave me away?"

"Your accent," she murmured, not daring

to move. Her gray hoodie had bunched up under her tweed jacket, but she didn't care. She liked having this strange boy's arms wrapped around her.

"That's a relief," he joked. "I'd hate to think I'd done something really stupid to make me stand out like some vile foreigner."

Hannah couldn't stop staring. "You're definitely not vile," she murmured. In fact, he was very well put together, from his sixties mod striped shirt to his navy blue cords.

"Yo, Hannah!" a male voice called from the locker across the hall. "Who's your new friend?"

Kyle Martinez's voice jerked Hannah back to reality. She froze, aware of what she must look like wrapped in this stranger's arms.

The new boy felt her body stiffen and instinctively dropped his arms to his sides. They both looked embarrassed.

"Um, hi, Kyle!" Hannah said, tugging both jackets down over her ribbed T-shirt. She pointed to the new boy. "This is, uh . . ."

Leaping to her rescue, the British stranger quickly shook hands with Kyle. "Dylan Saunders. Pleased to meet you."

"You from England?" Kyle asked.

"As a matter of fact, I am," Dylan replied. "My family moved here just three days ago."

"Welcome to Colorado, man," Kyle said as he pulled two chemistry books out of his locker and stuffed them in his blue North Face backpack. "I think you'll like it here. Red Rocks is a pretty cool school."

"I'm sure it must be," Dylan replied.

Kyle was one of the most outgoing guys at Red Rocks and a good friend of Hannah's. "So, how do you know Hannah?"

"I nearly frightened her to death just moments ago," Dylan replied.

Kyle raised an eyebrow, confused.

"I wasn't frightened," Hannah explained to Kyle. "I was startled and kind of lost my balance."

Kyle gave Hannah an *I don't get it* shrug and said, "Whatever." He swung his locker closed with the heel of his hand. "Catch you guys later."

As Kyle disappeared into the mass of students crowding the hall, Dylan turned back to Hannah. "So . . . it's Hannah, is it?"

"Yes." Hannah smoothed a stray blond

hair out of her face and tucked it back into her French braid. "Hannah Briggs."

"Well, Hannah Briggs, I'm extremely pleased to meet you."

"Me too." Hannah was suddenly aware that more than one girl in the hallway was watching her chat with Dylan. She quickly looped her cargo messenger bag over one shoulder. "I guess I'd better run."

Hannah closed her locker and started to hurry down the hall. She hadn't taken more than a few steps when she felt a tap on her shoulder.

"I hate to be a pain," Dylan said, jogging after her. "But I really *am* lost. Could you spare one more second to help me out with my schedule?"

"Oh, sorry, Dylan," Hannah said, with a giggle. "I forgot you were lost. Here, let me see your schedule."

Dylan handed her the printout. "Where I go to school in Hampstead Heath—it's a suburb of London—the classes are all on top of one another in the same decrepit building," he explained. "Here, it's a bit like university. Everything is spread out and terribly confusing."

Hannah studied Dylan's schedule. She could tell a lot about him just from reading his class lineup. He had AP statistics and physics on his schedule, which meant he was smart. He was registered for honors history of modern Europe, which meant that he had to be a senior. And he had to be a pretty confident guy, because he was signed up for advanced speech and debate.

Hannah realized she'd been staring a little too long at the class schedule. "Sorry," she said. "I was just checking out your classes. AP statistics." She nodded her approval. "Very impressive."

"Ah, yes. That appears to be the one I can't find, which is hardly impressive, is it?" Dylan shrugged sheepishly. A lock of his light brown hair fell loosely across his forehead.

"Since so few of our students take that class, the administration put it at the far end of campus. Out in Siberia," Hannah joked. "That's what we call the portables standing out by the big red rocks." Hannah pointed toward the exit. "It's through those doors. Just follow the sidewalk. When you reach the end, that'll be Mrs. Ortlip's classroom."

"I'll push off, then," Dylan said. He started to leave, then hesitated, fixing her with his dark green eyes. "You're not by any chance going my way, are you?"

"Um . . ." Hannah knew she should hurry to her modern American literature class, which was in the opposite direction, but she was really enjoying having an extremely cute boy focus all of his attention on her. Usually it was just the opposite. She did all the staring while boys focused their attention on her best friend, Rachel Truitt.

"Well, I do have a message to deliver to Mr. Tredwell," Hannah said, quickly glancing at the clock on the wall above the lockers. "He shares the portable with Mrs. Ortlip."

"Brilliant!" Dylan said. "Then I can escort you."

"Great." Hannah wasn't exactly lying. She did need to talk to Mr. Tredwell. He was the faculty sponsor for the outdoor club and she wanted to go over the schedule for their hike to Cathedral Rock next week. But that really could wait until after school.

The pair stepped through the carved wooden doors of Red Rocks' west wing into the cool October air. Golden leaves shimmered on the elm trees lining the covered walkway. Hannah walked alongside Dylan, matching his steps stride for stride. He was tall, maybe six-foot-two or -three. That was good. Hannah was no shorty herself. Five-foot-ten in her bare feet, and five-foot-eleven in her ever-present brown suede cowboy boots.

"So they really *do* wear cowboy boots out here in the West," Dylan remarked as they made their way down the covered walkway that led to the outbuildings by the red rocks. "My father assured me that custom was only practiced in Texas."

Hannah chuckled and kicked up one of her boots. "Cowboy boots are allowed in Colorado, too. I wear them because they're comfortable, and because I work part time at a stable."

Dylan's eyes lit up. "Then you're a genuine cowgirl?"

"Yes, if that means I ride horses," Hannah said, glancing sideways at Dylan. "No, if it means I herd cows. I don't think I've ever even touched a cow."

Dylan's face reddened. "I know I must sound a bit daft, going on about cowgirls and cowboy boots, but when my father informed me we were moving to Colorado, all I could picture was one big dude ranch." He tilted his head slightly. "You don't happen to live on a ranch, do you?"

Hannah shook her head. "Sorry to disappoint you, but I live in a regular old subdivision about a mile from here. It's called Mountain Air Estates."

Dylan grinned. "Sounds very healthy."

Hannah rolled her eyes. "Not even. Everyone drives an SUV or a pickup, or both. You can choke on the gas fumes in my neighborhood."

"At least out here you can hike to the top of some mountain peak and breathe clean air. In London some days you have to climb to the top of Westminster to get above the smog."

Hannah liked listening to Dylan talk. He was funny and smart, and every warning bell in her body was going off. Could a person truly fall for a complete stranger in just a matter of minutes? Yesterday Hannah would have said love at first sight was impossible. But today . . .

Brrrrring!

"Oh God, there's the bell!" Dylan said,

putting his hand under her elbow. His touch sent little jolts up her arm, like electricity. "Now I've made you late."

"No problem," Hannah said, as she tried to remember if the quiz in modern American literature was scheduled for today or tomorrow. "I'll just introduce you to Mrs. Ortlip, and then I'll hurry back to my class. My teacher, Mr. Baumbach, will be totally cool about it. I'll talk to Mr. Tredwell later."

They had come to the door of the portable at the far end of the campus. The statistics teacher was just getting up from her desk when Hannah stuck her head in the door. "Mrs. Ortlip?" she called. "This is Dylan Saunders. He's just moved here from England."

Her announcement set off a flurry of loud whispering, particularly in the back corner, where Toby Baldwin and her friends were sitting. Toby was what Rachel liked to call a "triple threat"—cute, smart, and rich. Hannah felt herself bristle. Dylan was her find and she didn't want anyone, particularly Toby, laying claim to him.

Mrs. Ortlip shook the newcomer's hand.

"Welcome to Colorado, Dylan. Let's see if we can find you a desk."

Toby's hand shot up. "Over here, Dylan." She crossed her legs and revealed several inches of thigh under her extremely tight denim skirt. "You can share with us."

Hannah was relieved to see Mrs. Ortlip direct Dylan to an empty desk in the second row. He would be sitting between burly John Wing and David Delgado, the science club president. Perfect!

Dylan touched her arm and said softly, "Thanks, Hannah."

Hannah wanted to be sure she'd see him again so she quickly whispered, "Our outdoor club meets on the quad at lunchtime. Come join us and I'll introduce you to the guys."

"It's a date," Dylan whispered back.

Date! That little word made her blush instantly. She was certain Mrs. Ortlip and the entire class was aware of it. Hannah waved stupidly, and stumbled backward out of the room.

Outside on the sidewalk she had to take a moment to remember where she was supposed to be. This new guy had really rattled her.

"Take a deep breath, Briggs," she told herself. "He's just a guy."

With the exception of Rachel, most of Hannah's friends were boys. But guy pals, not boyfriends. Even though she was a senior, Hannah had never been the dating type. If she went to a dance or out to a movie, she usually went with a group—which she liked. Or she went on double dates arranged by Rachel—which she hated.

It wasn't that Hannah had anything against dating. It was just that no boy had ever really interested her . . . until now, miraculously. And it had happened in an instant!

And now, as she tried to remember what planet she was on, Hannah understood at last what it was that had turned most of her friends into babbling idiots. Love, with a capital *L*.

All at once, wisecracking, levelheaded Hannah had that fizzy-pop feeling in her stomach. She wanted to giggle. She wanted to shout. She wanted to hop up and down and squeal like Toby Baldwin. Instead, she skipped all the way down the walk to the main building. Once she was in the hall, she went back to her normal no-nonsense pace and hurried to her class.

But something had truly changed in Hannah—and everyone was about to notice it.

2

Two hours later Hannah raced to the cafeteria. She didn't want to miss her "date" with Dylan. She grabbed her usual hamburger and carton of milk, then carried the tray through the cafeteria looking for him. She was craning her neck so hard that she nearly dropped her lunch tray twice.

Dylan was nowhere to be seen. Hannah walked up and down the aisles of long folding tables so many times that some of the kids began cracking jokes about it.

"If you jog while you eat, you'll get cramps," Wendy Simmons cracked.

"Oh, miss?" Ryan Merrill yelled. "They need a waitress at table thirteen!"

Finally Hannah decided to stand in the

glass double doors that opened out onto the quad, so she could check both inside and outside. But she had to move out of the way constantly to let students pass through. After ten minutes of waiting she had had enough.

"First date, and I've been stood up," Hannah muttered. She decided to join the rest of the outdoor club at their usual spot on the quad—the picnic table nearest the sculpture of a soaring bald eagle.

It had originally been a fountain, but when too many books, purses, and kids found their way into the water the first year the fountain was in use, the school decided to fill it in. Now the fountain was a flower bed with an eagle circling overhead. But kids still called it "the fountain."

Paul Hume, the club's redheaded clown, was up to his usual tricks, doing what he called "fun with lunch." Today that meant dangling a spoon off the tip of his nose. Hannah could hear Kyle Martinez counting slowly. The group was clearly timing Paul's stunt. He had his arms held out to keep his balance.

"Forty-seven, forty-eight," Kyle said,

staring at his Swatch. He caught sight of Hannah and didn't skip a beat. "Hi, Hannah-nine. Fifty, fifty-one, fifty-two . . ."

Paul moved just his eyes to look at Hannah. "Hannah Banana! Check this out!"

"Alert the media!" Hannah cracked as she slid her tray onto the picnic table across from Paul. "'Hot Dog' Hume has a spoon stuck on his nose."

"It's not stuck! I'm balancing it," Paul said, forgetting what he was doing and lowering his chin. The spoon hit the table. "Now you blew my record time!"

Noah Kass, dressed in his trademark rugby shirt and tan chinos, looked up from his food and cracked, "Hume, spoons are easy. Try a fork!"

Noah tossed him a fork and Paul caught it with one hand. He immediately jammed the prongs up his nostrils, and for a second the fork dangled in midair. Then it thunked onto the table.

Shaggy-haired Colby Allen, the only skateboarder in the group, was swallowing a large gulp of root beer when he saw Paul's fork stunt. Foaming soda shot out of Colby's nose and spattered his vintage U2 T-shirt, which made all the guys double over with laughter.

Normally Hannah would have laughed just as loudly as the rest of them. But she had other things on her mind. Like the new boy, Dylan. Where was he?

Noah waved his hand in front of her face. "Briggs, wake up. These clowns are funny and you haven't even cracked a smile."

Hannah blinked several times in confusion. "Sorry, guys. I'm looking for someone. He said he'd come to our meeting."

"He?" Paul repeated, leaning over the table toward her. "Who is this *he?*"

This was the moment when Hannah should have blown off Paul's teasing and called Dylan a he-man who was going to whip their girly butts. Instead she did something very un-Hannah-like. She blushed. Twice in one day!

Paul spotted it immediately. "Whoa! Hannah's got a boyfriend!"

"Do not!" Hannah said quickly.

"Do too!" Paul shoved his freckled face closer to hers.

"Not!" Hannah shot back, pressing her forehead against his forehead.

"Too!" Paul shouted into her face.

"Break it up!" Kyle grabbed Paul by the scruff of his CU sweathood and yanked him backward. "I want details. What's this guy's name?"

Hannah checked over both shoulders and lowered her voice. "His name is Dylan Saunders. He just moved here from England." She glared at Paul. "And he's *not* my boyfriend."

Paul leaned forward and whispered, "But you like him."

Hannah shrugged. "Yes. I mean, I just met him for five minutes. Gimme a break."

Colby punched Paul lightly on the shoulder. "Chill, will ya?"

"Yeah, Hume," Kyle said, punching Paul on the other shoulder. "This club could use some new members. Especially for that moment when we vote you off the island."

Paul tossed a napkin at Kyle. "Who was the guy that saved your butt on the Pinnacle Peak climb? *Moi.* This club *needs* me."

Paul was right, of course. Each member of the outdoor club brought something special to the group. Noah was the clear leader, but Paul was the guy with quick reflexes—something you liked to have on treacherous climbs. Small, wiry Kyle was the best climber, along with Hannah. Tall, thin Colby was the fun-loving peacemaker. Together they made a pretty tight unit.

Colby twisted the yellow Live Strong bracelet around his wrist and murmured, "Seriously, Hannah, if you've got your eye on some cool dude, we support you. I mean, it's about time. Am I right, guys?"

A chorus of male voices answered him.

Hannah covered her face with her hands. "Thanks for the support, but this is way over the top." She lowered her hands and explained, "I just invited this guy to our club meeting. That's all."

Right now Hannah was having serious regrets about having made the invitation. Luckily for her, the mention of "club" and "meeting" set the group back on track.

"Whoa," Noah said, checking his diving watch. "We've got about twelve minutes to do the logistics for the Cathedral Rock climb. Is everybody in?"

"Totally," Kyle replied, pulling out a dog-eared topographical map. "I've got the beta on the route we should take. Mr. Tredwell gave me it this morning."

Paul stroked his chin. "I'm thinking I'd like to bring Caitlin Debussy."

"Does she like climbing?" Hannah asked, surprised.

"No, but she likes me," Paul said with a wiggle of his eyebrows. "And what girl can resist watching this stud rappel down the side of a cliff?"

Hannah rolled her eyes. "If I know Caitlin, she's more of a shop-till-you-drop than a hike-till-it-hurts kind of girl. In fact, I clearly remember from PE that Caitlin hates to sweat."

Colby gave Paul a good-natured shove. "Who wants to watch you hotdog it down the side of a cliff?"

"Don't bring Caitlin," Kyle said stiffly. "She'll eat all the chocolate out of the trail mix and ask someone to carry her back."

"That's right!" Noah snapped his fingers and pointed at Kyle. "You dated Caitlin once or twice, didn't you?"

"Once or twice!" Hannah nearly choked on her hamburger. "Get serious. They were totally hooked up all last winter."

Hannah remembered more than one two-hour phone call with Kyle, listening to him drone on and on about Caitlin.

Paul winced. "Sorry, dude. I totally spaced that."

Kyle shrugged. "It's no big. I'm over her completely. But I'm serious about the trail mix. She's a chocoholic and a major princess."

Noah slammed his sports bottle on the table. "Then it's settled. Caitlin will sit out the Cathedral Rock climb."

"Ahhh," Paul whined.

Hannah leaned one elbow on the table. "I don't get it. What do you guys see in Caitlin Debussy? She's such a poser. She cakes on the makeup and wears too-high heels and those too-short minis. . . ."

"Exactly!" Paul said, touching his finger to his nose.

Hannah's jaw dropped. "You seriously like that?"

Paul nodded eagerly. Hannah looked at Colby and Kyle, who shrugged sheepishly. Only Noah hesitated.

"I like girls to be girls," Noah said carefully. "But I also like brains. Let's face it,

Paul, Caitlin's not the brightest star. . . ."

"And your point?" Paul countered.

Hannah took a sip of her milk. "So, Paul, if I were trying to get some guy's attention, you think I should wear minis, eyeliner, and talk like Jessica Simpson?"

Paul shrugged. "It couldn't hurt."

"Whoa! Time!" Colby held up his hands in a T formation. "Hannah, you shouldn't change. Ever. You're the best."

Kyle agreed. "It would be too weird to see you in makeup and heels and all that hot stuff."

"But you just said guys like that," Hannah said.

"Right," Paul agreed. He stuck his fork back up his nose and added, "But guys are idiots."

Hannah threw her hands in the air and sighed, "I give up."

"So soon?" a voice responded behind her. "We've only just begun to fight."

Hannah didn't need to turn around. She knew who it was by the accent. "Dylan, you made it!"

"Sorry to be so late." Dylan stood awkwardly at the end of the table. "I thought I had this school figured out, but I was dead wrong."

Hannah slid sideways to make room for him, giving Noah an extra-hard bump. "You haven't missed a thing, Dylan. Trust me."

Hannah made the introductions and Dylan shook hands with the guys in the club. Once they were done, Noah asked, "Are you a climber?"

"Social or recreational?" Dylan asked, taking a seat next to Hannah.

Hannah giggled a little too loudly, which caused Paul and Kyle to share some meaningful smirks.

"I've trekked on holiday," Dylan explained. "And done a bit of abseiling."

"Abseiling?" Paul repeated.

"That's the Brit word for rappelling," Noah explained to Paul. "Same bounce down the side of a rock face, just a different name."

"Rappelling," Dylan corrected himself. "But I've never really done any serious climbing with ropes and pitons, if that's what you mean."

"We've done some technical climbs," Kyle said. "But generally we just hike to some really high place and rappel down it."

"Brilliant," Dylan said, turning to smile at Hannah.

Colby nodded. "It's extremely cool."

"We're going up Cathedral Rock next Friday," Noah added. "Want to join us?"

"That would be fantastic," Dylan replied enthusiastically. "But don't I have to pass some sort of test to join the club?"

The boys exchanged quick looks. Hannah could see from the impish look in Paul's eyes that all sorts of wacky, humiliating pranks were buzzing through his brain.

"Don't even think about it!" Hannah muttered under her breath to Paul. He immediately slumped down with his head on the table like a defeated puppy.

Noah consulted his yellow pad. "We were just about to do food sign-up. You know . . . power bars, trail mix . . ."

"How do you feel about those little chocolate pieces in trail mix?" Kyle asked Dylan pointedly.

"I'm all for them," Dylan replied.

"Don't mind Kyle," Hannah explained, touching Dylan's arm. "His ex-girlfriend used to snarf up all the chocolate chips, and Kyle's never gotten over it."

"I see." Dylan nodded sympathetically at Kyle. "The less said about birds who eat your chocolate bits, the better."

"Birds, girls," Paul repeated with a laugh. "That's good."

Hannah glanced around the picnic table. All of her friends were smiling at Dylan. They liked him, that was clear. It just confirmed her own feelings about him, which were growing by the second.

With only a few minutes left in the lunch period, Noah hurried through the rest of the club's business. Paul agreed to bring the peanut butter, as always. Kyle took the trail mix, Colby took the Oreos, and Hannah promised to mix the lemonade. Dylan was assigned the job of bringing string cheese, which was new to him.

While they were planning rides, Hannah caught sight of her friend Rachel standing in the doorway of the cafeteria.

Rachel was wearing a winter-white, crocheted poncho over a curve-hugging Lycra dress in her favorite color—raspberry pink. Her long, dark brown hair was cut in a soft shag around her face. No doubt, Rachel was a knockout. Even the guys in the club paused a moment to reflect on Rachel's beauty.

"Skirt alert," Paul murmured.

Dylan turned to see where everyone was looking, and asked, "Who's that girl?"

"Rachel Truitt," Colby replied. "Red Rocks' designated babe."

At that moment Rachel caught sight of Hannah. She stood on tiptoe in her platform shoes and waved. Hannah waved back, remembering that she had promised to study for world religions with Rachel after school. Hannah half hoped that Rachel would forget, but no such luck. Rachel put her thumb and pinky to her ear in a *call me* gesture. Hannah nodded.

Meanwhile Paul and the rest of the guys in the club were making the standard "hottie" remarks about Rachel. Hannah was so used to it that she barely heard them.

Hannah would have liked to talk longer to Dylan, but the bell rang. That signaled the mad dash to the dishwasher's window to bus their plates. As they tossed their silverware in the plastic tub, Noah told Dylan to give any of the guys a call if he wanted some more information on the outdoor club.

"How can I find your numbers?" Dylan asked.

"The school directory," Kyle called as he looped his pack over his shoulder. "They probably gave you one in your welcome pack. It's got the phone numbers and e-mail addresses of all the students in school."

"Thanks, mate," Dylan said, with a wave. "I'll give it a look."

As the group dispersed Hannah shot a nervous glance at the clock. Her next class was Spanish III, and she could not be late. Señor Alvarez docked points for tardiness.

"Nice group of chums you've got there," Dylan said as he followed Hannah to the cafeteria exit.

Hannah shrugged. "They can be pretty raw sometimes, but they're basically good guys."

"Well, I certainly made the right choice, stopping at your locker this morning." Dylan smiled at her appreciatively. "Thanks, Hannah."

Dylan said her name in that cute British way, where it sounded like "Hanner"—and she loved it.

She would've liked to linger but the clock showed she had two minutes to sprint to the west wing.

"Listen, Dylan," she said, turning and jogging backward. "Gotta run. If I don't catch you later, call me!"

Hannah couldn't believe how bold she had been. She'd never asked a boy to call her. When Dylan looked confused, she pointed to the red-and-gold spiral notebook buried in his stack of books. "Use the directory. Hannah Briggs!"

"I'll do that," Dylan said. "Ciao!"

Hannah's feet and spirits were flying as she sprinted the length of the main hall in ten seconds flat.

3

Hannah turned her battered red Tacoma pickup into the driveway of her home in Mountain Air Estates. "Estates" was a grand way of saying lots of half-brick, half-wood split-level homes crammed into one small housing area. The upper level of Hannah's home was painted yellow with white shutters. Rachel's house across the street was a clone of Hannah's, except it was painted a pale pink with black shutters.

As she got out of the pickup Hannah could hear the happy barks of Sheila, her Australian shepherd, waiting at the door to welcome her home. She could also hear music blasting from Kirk Boyd's BMW as he dropped Rachel off in front of her house.

Kirk was one of the many guys who lined up each day after school, eager to give Rachel a ride home.

Rachel, cute as ever, bounced out of Kirk's car. "Sorry I can't ask you in," she said. "But I have an appointment that I really can't break." Then she leaned her head in the car and air-kissed Kirk. "Thanks, sweetie. You're the best."

Hannah could tell by the way Kirk revved his engine that he liked being called "sweetie" by Rachel. Kirk was probably certain Rachel had a major thing for him. Hannah knew better.

It was obvious to her that Rachel was just being nice to Kirk, just as she was to all of the boys who flocked around her. It wasn't really Rachel's fault. She had a way of making everybody she talked to feel special. Too often guys took her acts of kindness to mean much more than Rachel ever intended. Kirk was only the latest in a long line of Rachel admirers.

"Hannah Briggs!" Rachel called as Hannah opened her front door. "Fifteen minutes! You bring the books. I'll bring the party favors!"

On the surface that sounded like a great deal. In reality it meant that Hannah would be studying for both of them while Rachel nibbled the rice cakes, drank diet Snapple, and grooved to OutKast on the CD player. Hannah was better off studying by herself. But she had to admit that being with Rachel was lots more fun.

Rachel was ditzy and impulsive, and her life seemed to be filled with fun adventures. Of course, most of those adventures involved guys, but that made them even more interesting. Especially for Hannah, who hadn't gotten that side of her life on track.

"Don't forget the smoothies," Hannah called across the street. "You promised pineapple-strawberry."

"Hey, am I not the blender queen?" Rachel said, snapping her fingers and striking a pose. "I'm on it. Ciao, baby!"

Hannah kicked off her boots at the front door. She'd stopped at the Obstinate J Stables on her way home and mucked out three of the stalls. A new mare was moving in and she'd promised Ellie, the owner, that she'd help get her stall ready. Of course, once she'd cleaned out Fancy Girl's stall, she'd had to clean the stall for her horse, Bo Tie. And Bo's neighbor, Tuxedo, was making such a fuss that she cleaned his stall too. Her boots were filthy.

Sheila was so excited to see Hannah that she spun in circles, chasing her nonexistent tail and barking with pleasure.

"Hello, Sheila girl," Hannah said, kneeling down and giving her dog an affectionate hug. As usual, Hannah's entrance into her home set off a parade of animals.

First, Bongo, her mother's Jack Russell terrier, rocketed through the doggy door into the living room. He was followed by Sam, a muscular Siamese cat with a crooked tail. The cat and Bongo were inseparable.

Sonny, their African gray parrot, went wild, screeching, "Down, Bongo! Bongo, be quiet!" Lastly, Maizey, the family's ancient tabby cat, hobbled down the stairs from her sleeping place in Hannah's bedroom. Now that she was so old, her voice sounded more like an *awk* than a *meow*.

Hannah got some treats out of the pet cookie jar in the kitchen. Bongo, Sheila, and Sam promptly sat in a dutiful circle around her, looking up expectantly.

"Has everybody been good today?" Hannah asked as she dropped a bit of biscuit or kibble into each pet's mouth.

A voice answered from the laundry room, "If you call flipping over the kitchen garbage and dragging empty tuna cans and used coffee filters all over the family room 'good,' then these guys were gold medal winners."

"Hi, Mom," Hannah said, sticking her head in the laundry room. "I didn't know you were home."

Bonnie Briggs was folding bath towels and stacking them on the dryer. At a quick glance, she looked like Hannah's older sister—tall, thin, and blond. They even shared the same jeans and T-shirts, though Mrs. Briggs preferred Miss Sixty and Hannah leaned toward Abercrombie.

"Technically I'm not here," Mrs. Briggs replied. "I was doing some field work in Golden and thought as long as I was passing the house—"

"You'd stop in to do some laundry?" Hannah finished for her.

"No, no," her mother laughed. "I was going to pick up some gardening books to return to Rob in Golden, but then I saw the mess in the family room and started to clean it up."

"And while you were cleaning *that* up, you thought you'd do a load of clothes," Hannah concluded.

"Exactly." Her mother touched the tip of her nose with her finger. "And now I've got to run."

Hannah shook her head. Her mom was a staff botanist for the Denver Botanic Gardens. She was the coauthor with Rob Proctor of several gardening books and was in great demand as a landscape designer.

To Hannah, she was a walking contradiction. At work her mom was extremely organized; at home she was a complete scatterbrain. She had good intentions but often never completed whatever household chore she started. The odds were good that Mrs. Briggs would forget about the laundry still in the washer and it would almost mildew before anyone else in the family found it. The same thing happened on the cooking front. More than once Mrs. Briggs had put something on the stove and then left the house, completely forgetting about it. Luckily Hannah or her father usually caught her mistakes in time.

"Hannah," her mother called as she hurried toward the front door. "Help me find my bag, and then would you prepare dinner? I put some frozen lasagna on the counter. I'll try to be back in time to sit down with you and Dad."

"Here it is." Hannah handed her mother an overstuffed Denver Botanic Gardens canvas tote. "And here are your car keys and your camera."

"Oh, right!" Her mother kissed her on the cheek. "What would I do without my Hannah? Steady, reliable—"

"*Bor*-ing," Hannah finished, although her mom didn't hear her. Mrs. Briggs had already left the house and was still muttering to herself as she hopped into her green Subaru station wagon.

Hannah shut the door. "Steady" and "reliable" were not exactly words a teenage girl wanted to hear about herself. She would rather have been called impulsive, wild, or wacky—at least sometimes.

The phone rang, interrupting her thoughts.

"Where are you?" It was Rachel, the epitome of impulsive, wild, and wacky. Hannah could see Rachel through the front window, standing in front of her house. She had changed into her pink Uggs, cutoff sweats, and pink Phat Farm T-shirt. She held a blender full of frothy pink liquid in one hand and her cell phone in the other. "The drinks are ready."

"I'm on my way," Hannah said, waving at Rachel through the glass. "I have something I want to tell you."

"Hurry up, these smoothies can't wait," Rachel sang out, wiggling the blender in the air.

Hannah ran into the kitchen, put the frozen lasagna in the oven, and set the timer for an hour. She tucked the timer and two apples into her pockets and bolted out the front door with her messenger bag over her shoulder.

As Hannah crossed the road Rachel raised her blender and called, "Follow me." She led Hannah up the front steps and inside the house.

"Did you get a load of Denny Arndt today?" Rachel asked as they ran up the stairs to her room. "He was spinning donuts in his new Jeep Wrangler on the gravel behind the stadium after school. He was showing off for the girls."

"You mean *girl*," Hannah corrected. "Denny's had the hots for you for months." He'd even called Hannah a few times to see if she could help hook him up with Rachel.

"No, he doesn't," Rachel scoffed. "I hardly see him. Besides, you're changing the subject. Krytzer caught him and told him he'd be banned from the school parking lot if he ever did it again."

Mr. Krytzer was the vice principal and most feared man at Red Rocks High. He doled out punishment like candy.

"He's not the first guy who's risked the wrath of Krytzer for you," Hannah added. "You have to be more careful."

"What did I do?" Rachel protested. "I was just walking by."

Rachel kicked open the door of her bedroom with one foot, revealing possibly the messiest room on the planet. Certainly the messiest room in Mountain Air Estates.

"Rachel, call 911!" Hannah cracked. "Your room has been mugged." She kicked her way through the clothes piled everywhere on the retro pink shag rug. "I can't even find the floor."

Rachel sighed. "Oh, I know. I keep meaning to get to it, but it's just so . . . so *much*. Just move them out of the way."

"And put them where?" Hannah gestured toward the pink bed. "Your bedspread is covered with magazines. And some sort of food item has done a face-plant on the table next to your bed. It's lying there upside down."

"That's pizza. And it's not upside down, I just ate the cheese off the top." Rachel tossed the skirts and tops off her white wicker couch and onto the top of her dresser. "Ignore all that, and sit down and tell me your big news."

Just the mention of "news" made Hannah forget about Rachel's disaster area and focus on Dylan. She couldn't wait to tell Rachel about the handsome Brit.

"But first," Rachel cut in, as she pushed some makeup brushes aside on her dressing table and filled two wine goblets with strawberry smoothies, "let me tell you *my* news." Rachel handed Hannah a glass. "I found the perfect guy for you. He's cute, smart, and likes the outdoors."

Hannah opened her mouth to say something but Rachel held up the palm of her hand. "Wait, I'm not finished. Before you do the Hannah shut-down, hear me out."

"What do you mean, the Hannah shut-down?"

Rachel took a sip of her smoothie. "Oh, you know. You go all stiff and quiet, and then you tell me you're too busy with school, the outdoor club, and working at the stables, and you don't really have time for a boyfriend."

Hannah's jaw dropped. "Rachel! But it's true, I *am* too busy."

Rachel rolled her eyes. "Oh, come on, Hannah! You could find time for a boyfriend if you really wanted one."

Hannah took a big sip of her smoothie and set the glass on the table. "That's my point. I don't want one. You're the one who's boy crazy. Why do I have to be boy crazy too?"

"Because boys are fun!" Rachel said, opening up a bag of soy chips. "And if you'd just loosen up a little, you'd see that."

"I know boys are fun. Most of my friends are boys," Hannah explained for the umpteenth time. "But please stop trying to find me a boyfriend. Every time you do, it's a disaster."

"And whose fault is that?" Rachel countered. "We could have had a great time on that double date with Randy Stuart and Josh Ensign last week, but you barely cracked a smile the whole time."

"As you recall, you and Randy thought it would be fun to go bowling and Josh thought it was *not* fun, and so while you and Randy were laughing it up and throwing gutter balls, Josh was complaining to me. You know what he was groaning about? You."

"Me?" Rachel looked completely surprised.

"Yes, Rachel," Hannah sighed. "Josh liked you too and thought it was unfair that Randy was your date. After all, he"— Hannah paused to make little quotation marks in the air—"saw you first."

Rachel winced. "Why didn't you tell me?"

Hannah shook her head. "Because you wouldn't have listened. So who's this hunk that's perfect for me now?"

Rachel studied her French manicure, embarrassed. "Um . . . Kirk Boyd."

"Kirk?" Hannah gasped. "Oh, come on, Rachel! Kirk's totally into you. He doesn't even know I exist."

"That's not true," Rachel said. "I talked about you all the way home today. And he seemed really interested."

"Yeah, right. Kirk listened because he wants to be a dutiful boyfriend."

Rachel flopped across the magazines on her bed. "Okay, okay, forget Kirk. I'm sorry I even brought him up."

There was a long silence.

"I just want you to be happy," Rachel said simply. "I worry about you. You could be having so much fun. And—"

"Just out of curiosity," Hannah interrupted, "why did you think Kirk was perfect for me?"

Rachel's face brightened. "Because he works as a golf caddie on weekends and in the summer."

Hannah frowned in confusion. "But I don't play golf."

"No, but you are an outdoors freak and golf is totally outdoors."

Hannah stared at Rachel in stunned amazement. Then she burst out laughing. "You're right," she said. "We're perfect for each other. Give him my number. Have him call me. Better yet, I'll go over to the golf course and throw myself at him."

Rachel grabbed one of the pink satin pillows buried under the clothes on her bed and threw it at Hannah. "Oh, come on, don't be sarcastic. I'm just trying to help."

Hannah blew a stray hair off her forehead in exasperation. "You don't need to help. Besides, I met someone today who *is* totally perfect for me."

Rachel leaned forward expectantly. "Okay, girl, spill it!"

Ding dong!

Hannah looked around, confused. At first she thought it might be the oven timer in her pocket but it wasn't. "Does your doorbell ring like that?"

Rachel hopped off her bed and picked her way toward her desk in the corner. "It's not my door, it's my iBook. I've got mail." She gave Hannah an apologetic smile and said, "Let me quickly check this and then I want to hear all about Mr. Perfect."

Rachel tapped the space bar on her computer and scrolled down to check her mail. After a moment she murmured, "How weird."

"What is it?" Hannah asked.

"It's a love letter," Rachel replied.

Hannah picked her way across the huge pink bedroom, trying not to step on school books and clothing and leftover plates and glasses. "Who's it from?"

"I'm not sure." Rachel turned the iBook so Hannah could read it. "Here. Look."

Dear Rachel,

There you were in your white shawl at the door of the cafeteria with the afternoon light glowing all golden around you, like an angel. Brilliant! There I was in front of you, with my heart in my throat like a stupid prat. Wanted to say hello. Couldn't muster the courage. Found your e-mail in the school directory. Permit me to introduce myself.

I'm Dylan Saunders.

4

Hannah stared numbly at the words on the computer screen. A tight ache began to swell up in the back of her throat. Her eyes started to burn, and for one awful moment she thought she would cry.

Dylan Saunders, the first boy Hannah had ever really fallen for—her Mr. Right—was now Mr. Wrong. Dylan had a crush on Rachel. Just like every other boy at Red Rocks High. Just like every other boy in the entire world. It wasn't fair!

Hannah had never felt so disappointed in her life. Her knees wobbled under her as she looked around for a clear spot to sit down.

"Hannah, are you all right?" Rachel asked. "You look ill."

"I am," Hannah replied dully. "I just need to sit here for a second."

Rachel watched Hannah carefully as she shoved aside the pile of clothes on her bed. "Are you sure you're not going to throw up or pass out?"

"I'm sure," Hannah said, swallowing hard.

Rachel still looked worried.

"Really. It's nothing. It's gone." Hannah forced a bright smile. "Must've been a brain freeze from that smoothie or something."

"I hope so," Rachel said. "You really gave me a scare."

She gave Hannah a reassuring squeeze on the shoulder, then turned her attention back to the computer screen.

"This is such a sweet letter," Rachel said, after reading it again. "But who is Dylan Saunders?"

Hannah stared at the floor. Her answer came out in a dull monotone. "He's a new boy at Red Rocks. Just moved here. Three days ago."

Rachel spun around in her pink fuzzy desk chair. "You know him?"

"I met him today," Hannah said. "He came to the outdoor club meeting at lunch."

Rachel's eyes lit up. "Oh, *that* boy? The one sitting next to you at the picnic table by the fountain?"

Hannah nodded. "That's the one."

Rachel was getting excited. She hurried over and flopped down on the bed beside Hannah. "He was very cute. In fact, I remember wondering at the time who he was. I loved his cute blond hair."

"It's brown," Hannah corrected.

"That's right." Rachel snapped her fingers. "Shaggy brown hair and brown eyes."

Hannah shook her head. "Green. His eyes are green."

Rachel giggled. "Well, he was all the way across the quad. I didn't get close enough to see his baby greens."

"Blues," Hannah said. "It's 'baby blues.'"

Rachel put one hand on her hip. "I thought you just said his eyes were green."

"I did. But the phrase is 'baby blues.' I don't think it applies to green," Hannah explained. "In fact, the usual comment is 'emerald greens.'"

Rachel was thoroughly confused. "Whatever! The important thing is, he's a real hottie. And he's new."

Hannah looked up at her friend. "You know, I don't think you're going to like him. I mean, he's a real outdoorsy type, like Kirk Boyd. He may even golf, like Kirk."

"Who cares if he golfs?" Rachel said, with a careless wave of her hand. "I want to know his personality. What's he like?"

"Well, he's *very* different," Hannah said, deliberately trying to scare Rachel off. "Not like the rest of the guys at all."

"That could be a good thing," Rachel mused. "Different in what way?"

"For one thing, he's from England," Hannah said, ticking his differences off on one hand. "And he has an accent."

Hannah regretted her words instantly.

"He's English? And has an accent? Like Orlando Bloom?" Rachel hopped off the bed and wrapped her arms around herself in a hug. "I *adore* English accents!"

"So do I," Hannah groaned.

Rachel raced back to her computer. "I have to write him back ASAP!"

She sat down at the keyboard, her hands poised above the keys, then dropped them back into her lap. "Oh God. I don't know what to write." She looked at Hannah desperately. "He thinks I'm an angel. What would an angel say?"

"I don't know," Hannah said listlessly. "Tell him about yourself. Ask him about himself. Isn't that what they do on those dating services?"

Rachel put one hand back on the keyboard. Just as quickly, she withdrew it. "I can't write it. You write it."

"Me?" Hannah winced.

"Yes, you're the straight-A English student." Rachel dropped to her knees in front of Hannah and took her by the hands. "Write something poetic," she pleaded.

Hannah was in complete despair. She had hoped that just this once things would turn out differently and *she'd* get the guy. But that was clearly not in the stars.

"All right," Hannah grumbled, standing up. "I'll write your dumb letter."

"Thank you, thank you, thank you!" Rachel hopped to her feet and gave Hannah a big hug. Then she pulled out her office chair and helped Hannah sit down. "Here you are. Now . . . go for it!"

Hannah read the letter again, and then reread it—partly to torture herself, and partly to make the truth sink in. The truth was that she had no possible chance to be more than just a friend to Dylan, and she had to learn to accept it.

At last Hannah took a deep breath and typed in her reply.

> Dear Dylan,
>
> Let's get one thing straight: I'm no angel, though I do like harp music and those big fluffy clouds that float over the Colorado plains on summer days. I am also really into flying. Big planes are great, but I like the small ones best. Heard you're a British import (just like the Teletubbies). Welcome to Colorado!
>
> Rachel

Hannah finished the letter and hit SEND before Rachel could make any comments.

"Hannah!" Rachel slapped Hannah's shoulder. "You should have told him about me."

"I did," Hannah replied.

"But that's not me," Rachel pouted. "That's you. I hate flying, especially in small planes."

"I doubt he's going to take you flying,"

Hannah said, still staring at the computer screen.

"And what's with the Teletubbies?" Rachel added. "That thing that little kids were into? I had no idea they were British."

"So you've learned something new," Hannah replied.

"But I would never have said any of that," Rachel insisted.

Hannah stood up. "So write him back and say your friend just sent that e-mail by accident."

Rachel put both hands on the hips of her cutoff shorts. "I can't do that. He'll think I'm an airhead."

"Look, are we going to study for world religions, or what?" Hannah asked, changing the subject.

Rachel picked up a silver chiffon scarf from the pile of clothes lying on the floor by her nearly empty closet and danced around the room. "I can't study now. I'm too excited. Damon could write back at any moment."

"It's Dylan!" Hannah said, a little too loudly. "How can you forget that?"

Rachel stopped dead in her tracks. "Sorry,

Hannah. I just forgot the guy's name."

This would have been the perfect moment for Hannah to confess to Rachel her true feelings about Dylan. After all, Rachel didn't know him yet. She couldn't even get his name straight.

But Dylan hadn't written to her. He'd written to Rachel.

"I'm sorry, Rachel," she said, closing her notebook and gathering up her study supplies. "I don't feel too good. Maybe I'm catching something."

"Oh, sweetie, I'll fix you a peppermint tea," Rachel said.

"That's okay," Hannah said. "I'm just going to go home."

Rachel pulled open the top drawer of her dresser. It was the only one that wasn't already open. "I've got just the thing to make you feel better," she said, sorting through sunglasses, sunscreen, headbands, and bottles of perfume. Finally she held up what looked like a beanbag pillow in the shape of a horseshoe.

"This is divine," she said. "It's filled with lavender and rice, or something. Anyway, you put it in the microwave, heat it up, and wrap it around your shoulders. It will make you relax and help get rid of that cold."

Hannah, who was nowhere near having a cold, started to feel bad watching Rachel fall all over herself trying to make her feel better. Luckily the cell phone rang, playing an electronic version of "Twinkle, Twinkle, Little Star," which put a stop to Rachel's home remedies.

"Omigod, it's Bryan Meeker," Rachel said, checking the caller ID readout. "He wants to go to the new Adam Sandler movie at Tinseltown Theater this Friday."

"And?" Hannah said.

"Well, like, he's cute, but not like A-list cute," Rachel said, hopping up and down anxiously.

The phone continued to play the familiar children's song. "Aren't you going to answer?" Hannah asked.

Rachel held the phone out in front of her, like it was covered in germs. "I don't really want to go. I don't know what to say."

"Say no," Hannah replied logically.

"I can't do that," Rachel whispered, as if Bryan could hear her. "That would hurt his feelings."

Hannah shrugged. "He'll just keep calling."

The phone stopped. A moment later it rang again.

"See?" Hannah said.

"I need an excuse, fast," Rachel said, looking at Hannah desperately.

"Well, um, tell him you're coming with me to the football game on Friday."

Rachel heaved a huge sigh of relief. "Thank you, Hannah—you're a doll!" Then she put the phone to her ear and said brightly, "Hi, Bryan. I'm so glad you called."

Hannah crossed her legs and rested her chin in her hand to listen.

"Oh, sweetie, I'm so sorry, I totally spaced that," Rachel said. "I already made plans to go to the football game with Hannah. Yeah, I know. I really wanted to see that movie, too."

Hannah winced. She knew that would keep Bryan dangling. He was sure to ask her out for the next night.

"Saturday?" Rachel looked at Hannah and frowned. "Oh, gee, Bryan, I, um, can't."

Hannah gave her a thumbs-up. Rachel wasn't being exactly straightforward with her answer, but at least she wasn't leading the boy on.

As Rachel artfully changed the subject by asking Bryan about homework in their history of rock-'n'-roll class, Hannah thought about what it really meant to be Rachel's best friend.

In kindergarten it was so simple and clear. They shared everything. Hannah helped Rachel figure out how to do things, like roller-skating and tree climbing. And Rachel was always there to smooth the way on the playground for shy Hannah.

Then in middle school things changed. Suddenly a big part of their friendship consisted of Hannah being Rachel's middle person. Boys called Hannah to see if Rachel liked them. It was Hannah's job to call Rachel to see how she felt, then call the boy back with Rachel's answer.

Luckily, when they reached high school, the boys were usually confident enough to make their own calls to Rachel, and Hannah could focus on her own life.

Hannah cocked her head, wondering why she had let herself be Rachel's messenger girl for all those years. Maybe she liked being in the thick of all the romantic turmoil of Rachel's life without having to be upset herself. It also gave her a chance to get to know some of the guys. In fact, her friendships with half the guys in the outdoor club dated back to those earlier messenger days.

"What are you smiling at?" Rachel asked, as she clicked off her cell phone.

Hannah sat up with a start. "I was just thinking about the old 'I love Rachel, does she love me?' days of middle school."

Rachel looked confused. "What do you mean?"

Hannah flopped back on a pile of laundry at the foot of Rachel's bed. "Come on, Rachel. You remember when everyone had a crush on you and they wanted me to call you and find out if you liked them back."

Rachel nodded her head. "Yeah, I remember. I also remember it was a two-way street. I got as many calls about you."

"Me?" Hannah grabbed a pair of socks from under her head and threw them at Rachel. "Get serious."

"I am totally serious," Rachel said. "Jonathan Hogan, Colin Burrows, Troy

McKee. All those guys were madly in love with you."

"Really?" Hannah sat up. She vaguely recalled being aware of a time when those guys seemed to be hanging around more than usual. "But I don't remember them calling you about me."

Now it was Rachel's turn to toss the socks back at Hannah. "Come on! Chip Dupont called me for a full week, begging me to call and find out if you liked him. So finally I did."

"What did I say?" Hannah asked.

"You said, 'What's the point? We're only in sixth grade.'"

They both laughed out loud.

"I was right," Hannah remarked. "I mean, we were just kids. What did 'going out' mean back then? I guess I thought I was too young to be dating."

"You could have met him at the movies," Rachel pointed out. "Or gone ice-skating with the rest of the gang."

"But that's not really going out," Hannah pointed out. "That's just doing stuff with a guy."

"That's exactly what you said then,"

Rachel said, shaking her head. "I can't believe you don't remember."

Hannah's long blond braid had gotten messed up when she had lain down on the bed. As she rebraided it she said ruefully, "I remember being this big loser that no guy ever looked at twice."

Rachel nearly choked on her drink. "Excuse me? Were you in a coma in middle school? All sorts of guys liked you, including Noah Kass."

When Hannah look startled, Rachel cried out in exasperation, "Don't tell me you've forgotten about Noah? He used to sneak over to your house and spell out messages with plastic forks on the front lawn."

"Oh, that's right," Hannah chuckled, thinking about the president of the outdoor club. She and Noah had been friends for so long that she had forgotten there'd been a time when they might have liked each other as more than friends. "I had a big crush on Noah, too," she murmured.

"What! You never admitted that!" Rachel gasped. "Why didn't you say anything?"

Hannah rose to her full height of five feet, ten inches. "Because as you recall, I was this tall in eighth grade. Noah was a shrimp then. I felt like a giant around him."

"So? He towers over you now." Rachel shook her head at her friend. "Just think, all these years you could have been going out."

"I'm glad we didn't," Hannah said firmly. She liked her relationship with Noah. They often went hiking together. He told her about his dating disasters, and she listened sympathetically. He was more of a brother than a friend.

Rachel cocked her head. "I don't get it. Noah seems like the perfect guy for you." She started to empty the rest of the blender into her glass when suddenly she gave a shriek. "Perfect guy! I just remembered. You met Mr. Perfect today!"

Hannah's eyes widened in surprise. She had almost forgotten all about the Dylan mess. "Did I?"

"That's what you said."

"I did?" Hannah asked, trying to avoid answering.

"Yes, you did. You were standing right there." She pointed to a spot in the middle of a pile of her skirts. "Who is he? Come on. Dish!"

Hannah licked her lips, trying to think. "Um, I don't actually know his name," she lied. "I just saw him. He was, um, at the stables. And he was riding a horse."

"That's it?" Rachel's shoulders slumped in disappointment. "Did you talk? How old is he?"

"No. We didn't talk. I don't know his age. He could be twenty."

Rachel grimaced. "Twenty. That's not perfect. That's old. Too old." She gave Hannah a knowing nod. "You need to confine your perfect guy search to high school. Preferably Red Rocks."

"We know everyone at Red Rocks," Hannah protested.

"New guys come to school every once in a while," Rachel replied. "Like that Dylan guy. You could find someone like him."

"Yeah." Hannah shrugged.

"Dylan could be an ax murderer, for all we know," Rachel said, wiggling her eyebrows. "A very cute one," she added. "But we'll know more about him as soon as he writes me back."

The mention of another e-mail from Dylan to Rachel made Hannah's spirits plummet. She couldn't bear the thought of seeing Dylan find out that she was Rachel's friend. She had gotten all mushy over Dylan, asked him to call her, and then he had sent *Rachel* a love letter. It would be middle school all over again. Agony!

Ding! This time the bell was Hannah's oven timer. As she gathered her books— which they hadn't even opened—she made a decision. From that moment on she'd have nothing to do with Dylan. If he wrote Rachel back, she wouldn't read the letter. She wouldn't even talk to him at school. She could just avoid Dylan and pretend that he never existed. It was the best way. In fact, it was the *only* way.

5

"Hannah, wait up!"

Hannah was hurrying across the front lawn to the entrance to Red Rocks High when she heard Dylan's voice behind her. She didn't turn around. It was Day One of her "Avoid Dylan" plan. Unfortunately school hadn't even started yet and he was already calling her name. In that cute accent of his.

"I say, Hannah! It's me, Dylan." His voice sounded confused.

Hannah couldn't resist looking at him, just once more. *I'm such a wimp,* she thought as she turned around to say hello.

Dylan stood with his books on his hip, looking like a back-to-school ad in his Ben

Sherman shirt and Tommy jeans. His face lit up in a warm smile, adding sparkle to his already devastatingly good looks.

"This was a big mistake," Hannah murmured under her breath. "I should have kept on walking."

"Thought for a moment you were giving me the brush," Dylan said as he joined her on the lawn.

"Why would I do that?" Hannah tried to keep her voice light and impersonal. "You're the new kid."

"Maybe I've got that desperately needy air," Dylan said, with a waggle of his head. "Which can be a bit of a turnoff for anybody."

"I don't think you have to worry about that." Hannah looked straight into his emerald green eyes. They weren't just emerald green, she noticed. They had a hint of blue, too. Maybe it was the blue and green stripes on his shirt that set them off that way. "I, um . . ." Her voice drifted off.

"You um?" Dylan repeated.

Hannah shook her head a little too emphatically, and the end of her ponytail slapped her in the face. This was ridiculous.

Less than a half hour into "Avoid Dylan" and here she was, drooling over the color of his eyes while blinding herself with her own ponytail.

"Dylan, my man!" Kyle Martinez jogged up from the direction of the parking lot and slapped Dylan on the back. "Is Hannah giving you the 4-1-1 on Red Rocks? This girl knows it all."

"Yeah," chimed in Paul Hume, who had appeared on Dylan's other side. "It's hard to believe that someone so hot could have brains, too!"

Kyle made an overexaggerated point at Hannah from behind his hand as he whispered to Dylan, "Major hottie."

"Hottie!" Colby repeated as he joined the gang gathered on the front lawn. "Are you guys talking about Hannah Banana? She, like, defines the word babe."

"Cut it out!" Hannah straight-armed Colby in the chest and made a face at Kyle and Paul. "You guys must be having some kind of mass hallucination."

Paul clapped Dylan on the back again. "Don't listen to her," he said with an over-hearty laugh. "She's just being modest. She's got so many guys after her, we have to act as her crossing guards."

Kyle shoved Paul. "Bodyguards, not crossing guards," he explained to both Dylan and Paul.

"Oh, really?" Dylan smiled bravely but was clearly confused by what was going on.

"Okay. What gives?" Hannah demanded, putting her hands on her hips.

Kyle stepped behind Dylan and gave Hannah a *zip your lip* gesture. Meanwhile Paul threw up his hands in exasperation.

Suddenly the lightbulb flicked on in Hannah's brain. Her friends weren't making fun of her; they were trying to help her. They knew she liked Dylan and were doing their unsubtle best to make sure he would like her, too.

It was an awfully sweet gesture but the actual result of their efforts was that Hannah had never felt so humiliated in her life. She had to make them stop *now.* The only way she could think of to do that was to let Paul and the others know the painful truth.

"Dylan has already found his own hottie," she announced, trying to make her voice sound playful and teasing. "And I know who it is. Rachel Truitt."

Dylan looked flustered, and his cheeks reddened. "Word certainly does travel fast out here in the West."

Hannah pretended to hold a cell phone to her ear. "I heard it by *phone-y* express."

Dylan chuckled and nodded his head. "Very good, that." He turned to Colby and joked, "Hannah is a hottie *and* a wit, to boot."

Colby didn't return Dylan's laugh. A sour look clouded his face. "Rachel?" he repeated. "You like *Rachel*?"

"I don't really know her at all," Dylan replied uncertainly, having caught Colby's expression. "But you must admit she is quite attractive."

"Rachel is totally hot," Paul agreed emphatically. He patted Dylan on the shoulder. "Awesome choice."

Kyle and Colby smiled sadly at Hannah. She didn't know which was worse, being publicly passed over by Dylan, or seeing the pitying looks on her friends' faces. Somehow Hannah found the will to put on a brave face.

"Well, Dylan, it was good seeing you," she said, smiling. "Let me know if there's anything I can do to help—"

"Actually, there is," Dylan cut in. "I need a lift home from school today. Any chance I might catch one with you?"

From their spot behind Dylan the guys were shaking their heads and giving Hannah giant signals to say no. But once again she couldn't resist. "Um . . . sure, Dylan. I have to stop by the stables first, but—"

"If it's not too much of a bother," Dylan interjected, "I'd love to take a look at your horses."

"Fine. No problem." Still wearing her frozen smile, Hannah backed up the sidewalk toward the front entrance to Red Rocks High. "I'll meet you in the parking lot after school. Three o'clock. Don't be late."

The instant she turned away, her smile turned into a frown. "So much for the 'Avoid Dylan' plan," she scolded herself. "Now I'm not only talking to him, I'm chauffeuring him around. Mortifying."

When the last bell rang six hours later, Hannah was already in the parking lot. She

had left journalism class early to clean out
her truck. There wasn't much she could do
about the torn leather seats, but at least she
could dump the empty Burger King drink
cups into the trash and wash off the dashboard. It was caked with an inch of red dust
from the dirt road that led to the stables.

Usually she changed into her work
clothes in her truck. Today, Hannah had
slipped on her torn Guess jeans and olive
green V-neck T-shirt in the girls' room
before heading out to her pickup. She threw
on her blue work shirt and leaned her head
back against the driver's seat to wait.

Twice during the day Rachel had cor-
nered Hannah to complain that Dylan
hadn't e-mailed her back. Rachel was certain
it was Hannah's "I'm no angel" comment
that had turned him off.

Hannah didn't know what to say to her
friend. How could she tell Rachel that
secretly she hoped Dylan *had* changed his
mind about Rachel? That he now realized
Hannah was the obvious choice for a girlfriend?

"Asleep at the wheel?" a voice called
through her passenger window.

Hannah bolted upright in the seat.

It was Dylan.

"Caught me daydreaming," Hannah said sheepishly. She tried to regain her composure as she leaned across the seat to throw open the passenger door. "Hop in."

He slid onto the seat and clouds of dust ballooned out of the worn leather cushion. Hannah grimaced. She'd remembered to dust the dashboard but not the seats.

"Sorry about that," she said, as Dylan waved away the dust.

"Not to worry," he reassured her. "I'm all right, really." As Hannah pulled out of the parking lot, Dylan confessed, "I know I may sound like a right idiot, but ever since I was a tot I've wanted to ride in a lorry—er, truck, I believe you call them."

"Oh, come on," Hannah cried. "You can't seriously tell me you've never been in a pickup before."

Dylan put his hand on his heart. "I swear to you, this is my very first outing in a . . . truck of any sort."

"So what do people drive in England?" Hannah asked. "In Colorado if you don't drive a truck, you drive an SUV."

Dylan nodded. "So I've noticed. But those vehicles are—how shall I put it?—a bit much for London driving. Our cars are quite a bit smaller on average than yours. It's because the roads are so much narrower."

"Why's that?"

"Parts of our towns and cities are hundreds of years old," he explained. "The streets were narrower in those days. Our cars—even our trucks—have to fit into some pretty tight places."

"Makes sense," Hannah said.

"Of course, most kids like you and me don't even have licenses in England. Or cars, for that matter."

Hannah hooted with laughter. "Now you *are* kidding me, right?"

Dylan shook his head. "No. We don't need them, really. Between the tube, the bus, and the taxis, you can get just about anywhere."

"The tube?"

"Oh. Sorry. I believe you call it the subway."

"So you don't drive?" Hannah asked.

"Oh, yes," Dylan said quickly. "Got my license this past year, as soon as I turned seventeen."

"Then why aren't you driving here?"

"I am. I do. Drive, that is. But on a scooter. A Vespa. Very classic, very retro." He grinned and added, "It's a bit easier to handle than a car. And I am having a spot of trouble adjusting to the way people drive here."

"Oh?"

"You Yanks drive on the wrong side of the road." He shook his head sheepishly. "I just can't get used to it." He made a veering motion with his hand to the left side of the road. "I seem to gravitate to that side of the roadway. Force of habit, I guess."

"If you ever offer me a ride home, remind me to just say no," Hannah said with a grin.

They had left the city limits of Golden behind and headed out Highway 26 toward the Obstinate J Stables.

"Hold on," Hannah warned as she made a hard turn onto a dirt road and the truck lurched over a huge bump. "We're now entering land mine territory."

"Land mines?" Dylan looked alarmed.

"Potholes," Hannah explained, pointing at the deep ruts and gullies in the dirt road. "This road is pockmarked with them."

Dylan stretched his arm across the back

of the seat as they bounced up the dusty road to the Obstinate J. Off in the distance, a red-roofed farmhouse and matching horse barns, bordered by lines of white clapboard fences, were faintly visible.

"It's really quite lovely," Dylan commented as they passed the ripening wheat fields stretching out from either side of the road. "Do you come here every day?"

"Sometimes I skip Sundays," Hannah replied. "But the more I work, the less I have to pay to board my horse, Bo. So, basically, I live here."

"Back home, I did quite a bit of riding on the heath," Dylan said. "It's rather tame compared to all of this. All very straight-laced and formal."

Hannah's eyes lit up. This was the first boy she'd liked who actually rode horses. "Would you like to go riding sometime?"

Dylan looked her straight in the eye and murmured in a husky voice, "That would be lovely."

His words sent goose bumps dancing up Hannah's arms. Once again she toyed with the idea that he might have changed his mind about Rachel. But no such luck.

"Does Rachel ride?" he asked.

Hannah hoped her face didn't register what she was feeling inside—enormous disappointment. "Rachel? On a horse?" She laughed breezily. "You couldn't get her near one. They're far too big and dirty and uncomfortable."

"Oh." Dylan's face fell. "Too bad."

"Rachel doesn't even like big dogs," Hannah continued as they rattled over the cattle guard and through the front gate of the Obstinate J Stables. "That's why her family has a Yorkie. You know, those little yappy dogs?"

Dylan winced. "Yes, I know the breed. They look like small toupees skittering across the floor."

Hannah started giggling. She couldn't help herself.

Dylan laughed too, but quickly stopped. "Aside from not being a big animal fan, Rachel seems to be a quite smart and fun girl," he commented.

Hannah rolled her eyes. "Yeah, tell me you were attracted to her mind."

Dylan actually blushed. "All right," he confessed. "On the totally superficial front, I think she's a knockout. But I also truly enjoyed her e-mail."

Hannah vowed secretly never to write another note for her friend. "Okay, I'll admit Rachel is pretty," she said. "And she's very energetic and flirty, which most of the boys say is fun."

"Most of the boys?" Dylan repeated.

"Well, she burns through a lot of guys," Hannah said with a shrug. "They get crushes on her and she flirts with them for a while, and then moves on to the next guy."

Hannah pulled the truck up beside the largest horse barn and wondered if that sounded catty or just truthful. Whichever it was, she hoped her words might discourage Dylan from pursuing Rachel.

They didn't. He took it as a challenge.

"Once I pluck up the courage to actually talk to her in person," Dylan said, "I'll try not to be too much of a wally."

"Wally?" Hannah cocked her head.

"You know, a stupid prat," Dylan explained. "Someone who's incredibly stiff and boring."

"Oh." Hannah flicked off the engine and set the parking brake. "All right, Wally, we're here. Let me show you around."

As Hannah got out of the truck, Dylan protested, "Now, Hannah, that's not fair. I can call myself a wally, but you can't."

"Oh, yeah? Watch me, Wally," Hannah chuckled as she led him into the horse barn and down the center aisle between the stalls.

Several horses stuck their noses over their stall doors to say hello. The first was a delicate Arabian. Her face was white and lightly dotted with gray.

"She's a beauty," Dylan said, patting her muzzle and running his hand down her neck. Hannah could tell by the way he handled the mare that he really did know his way around horses.

"That's Fancy Girl," Hannah said. "She's the new kid on the block, just like you."

Dylan leaned in close to Fancy Girl and murmured, "Let's hope you find someone as nice as Hannah to make you feel at home."

That should have made Hannah feel wonderful. Instead, it made her feel like the one thing she didn't want to be: Dylan's buddy. She continued down the stalls, pausing to pass a sugar cube into the mouth of each horse as she went by. She always kept a supply of them in her shirt pocket.

When they got to the last stall, a big bay was impatiently kicking at the door and nodding his head up and down. "Who's this handsome fellow?" Dylan asked.

Hannah swelled with pride as she wrapped her arms around her horse's neck. "This is Bo Tie. Bo for short," she said, burying her face in his mane. "Bo, meet Dylan."

Hannah watched Dylan as he stroked Bo's neck. He was very respectful; he acknowledged that Bo was a big, powerful being. Hannah could tell that Bo liked and trusted Dylan, too. Bo had a way of pressing his nose against your shoulder that showed that.

While Dylan got acquainted with her horse, Hannah went over to the feed bins. The oats were in a rolling container. The sound of her hand touching the handle set off a series of whinnies in the barn. Six heads appeared over the stall doors. Hooves thumped against wooden planks. In the far stall, Tuxedo, a huge black-and-white gelding, paced and snorted anxiously.

"What on earth's going on?" Dylan asked. He turned to look at all the horses, who were craning their necks in Hannah's direction.

"It's chow time," she laughed. "And these beasts are hungry."

"I'd best help you, before there's a riot," Dylan cracked.

He pushed the feed bin between stalls while Hannah carefully measured out the feed for each horse. While the horses ate, Hannah grabbed a wheelbarrow and a shovel and moved down the center aisle again, scooping up horse manure. This was the point where most of Hannah's friends wandered off to look at the goats, or check out the rest of the stables. But not Dylan.

"If you've got a spare shovel, I'll help," he offered. Hannah was only too happy to give him hers. She hurried into the tack room to get another shovel. She paused at the door to watch Dylan at work. He looked totally at home in the stables.

"It's not fair," Hannah murmured, as she grabbed a pair of work gloves. Dylan was her perfect match, but he couldn't see it.

After they'd mucked out the stalls and finished dumping the contents of the wheelbarrow in the compost heap, they took a break. Dylan smiled in admiration at Hannah. "You look like a real cowgirl—without the cows."

Hannah cocked her head. "Is that a good thing?"

Dylan chuckled. "Oh, yes. A very good thing. Back home we have this idealized version of the American cowgirl as a strong, capable beauty who can handle anything." He shrugged. "You fit the bill."

Hannah stared at him for a long time. "I think you've been watching too many reruns of *Dr. Quinn, Medicine Woman.*"

"Quite possible," Dylan said, laughing. "But you can't blame me. Don't you Americans think that England's chock-full of stuffy butlers bowing and scraping and saying things like 'Yes, madam. Right away, madam'?"

Hannah raised an eyebrow. "Uh . . . no."

Dylan shoved his hands in his pockets. "Then you must think I'm a lunatic."

"A complete lunatic," Hannah replied with a straight face.

He scraped at the red dirt with the toe of his shoe. "Well, that's that, then. I suppose I'll have to walk home."

"Don't be silly," Hannah replied, striding toward her red pickup. "I'll give you a ride. But you have to ride in the back."

"Thanks. That's awfully big of you," Dylan said in an overexaggerated, stiff-upper-lip style.

He started to climb into the flatbed of the truck, but Hannah caught hold of his shirt. He spun around, catching hold of her waist to steady himself. His face was only inches from hers. "We've got to stop meeting like this," he murmured.

Hannah would have liked to freeze that moment in time and stay that way forever. Unfortunately her cell phone began to ring. She tried to ignore it, but Dylan said, "Are you going to answer that?"

"Uh, yeah." Hannah reached her arm through the truck window and picked up her phone as Dylan crossed around to the passenger side. She saw the caller ID readout and her heart sank. "Hello, Rachel."

"Hannah, guess what?" Rachel squealed into the phone. "He wrote back!"

Hannah stepped away from the truck and whispered, "He did?"

"Yes, and you have to come read it, immediately."

Hannah looked back over her shoulder at Dylan, who was waiting for her inside the truck, and sighed heavily. "I'm a little busy at the moment."

"Is this horse business?" Rachel asked.

"Sort of," Hannah replied noncommittally.

"Finish that up and come read this letter. It's really long. You're going to like it."

The last thing in the world Hannah wanted to do was go to Rachel's house and read a letter from Dylan. But curiosity got the better of her. After all, she reasoned, he was really responding to *her*. She had written the letter, and Dylan had said he liked it. "Okay, I'll come over," she said. "After I finish my work and take a friend home."

"Friend?" Rachel repeated. "What friend?"

"Bye, Rachel," Hannah sang into the phone as she clicked off.

As they bounced down the rutted dirt road back toward Golden, she couldn't help laughing at the irony of her situation. Here she was, driving the boy of her dreams home so she could race to her friend's house to read his love letter to her best friend, not her. Life was bizarre!

6

Dear Rachel,

Yes, I'm a British import, though I don't quite fancy the Teletubbies. I'm more of a Crank Yankers kind of fellow. So why am I here? My dad's been sent by his company to work with people at the Colorado School of Mines on an engineering project.

I was sorry to leave my mates in England, especially in my last year in Sixth Form. But the students at Red Rocks are incredibly friendly. I'm looking forward to hiking the Rockies and reading extremely important books like *A Separate Peace* and *Lord Jim* whilst sitting next to a mountain lake and watching cougar, elk, and bighorn sheep frolic in the meadows. I'm sure they don't *all* frolic together. Now that I think of it, I'd say the cougars are more lurkers than frolickers.

I like nature, but I'm also very keen on the city life. Back in London, we would often meet up at the cafés by the Thames, then go to a club or two.

Now you know something about me. Tell me about you.

Dylan

P.S. My dad's got his pilot's license. I'm sure he'd love to take you up for a spin over the Colorado plains.

When Hannah read the last line, she burst out laughing.

"What's so funny?" Rachel called from inside her closet. Her mother had declared her room a toxic waste dump and ordered Rachel to clean it up immediately.

"Dylan's father is a pilot," Hannah called. "I think that's incredibly funny."

Rachel crawled backward into the room. Her thick dark hair was pulled into a wild ponytail on top of her head. She clutched a small broom and dustpan, and beads of sweat dripped down her nose, even though she was wearing her shortest shorts and a sports bra to clean in.

"That's so not funny," Rachel said, blowing a strand of damp hair out of her face. "I told you I hated flying."

"Tell him you just remembered you only like big planes," Hannah said with a grin.

Rachel tossed the broom at Hannah. "Then he'll write back to break the news that his dad just bought a jumbo jet."

Hannah leaned back in the desk chair with her hands behind her head. "Make up an excuse for why you can't go," she said. "You're good at that."

Rachel was pulling high heels, dirty clothes, and several dirty plates from under her bed. She stopped for a second and gave Hannah a quizzical look. "I hope you don't mean that I'm really good at lying," she said, examining one particularly old dish that could have been caked with meat loaf or chocolate cake.

"I wouldn't call it lying," Hannah replied.

"But somehow you manage to say 'no' in a 'yes' way that keeps guys hanging on."

"Not on purpose! I just hate it when they get all hurt, and then walk around school like sad-eyed puppy dogs." Rachel shoved the plate of mystery food back under the bed. "Oooh. This cleaning is making me crazy. This is *my* room. I should be able to do what I want in here."

Rachel stomped over to her closet, grabbed ten hangers, and threw them on the bed. One by one, she began to hang up the skirts and blouses strewn across the carpet.

"I suppose I should help you," Hannah said without getting up from her chair. "But I'm not sure what's clean or what's dirty."

"It's all clean," Rachel said. "I was in a hurry this morning and accidentally knocked these onto the floor."

"Wow!" Hannah eyed the enormous pile of clothes with dismay. "That's some acci-dent."

Rachel stuck her tongue out at Hannah. "Don't give me any grief." She walked to the door and shouted into the hall, "I get enough from my mother!" To emphasize her point, she slammed the door. It made a deafening boom, much louder than she'd expected.

"Oops." Rachel winced and stood still with her eyes shut.

A moment later her mother's voice called out from down the hall. "Breaking your bedroom door will not win you any favors!"

"See what I have to put up with?" Rachel whispered to Hannah.

Hannah burst out laughing. "Rachel, your mom wins the saint-of-the-year award for letting you mess up your room like this."

"What?" Rachel protested. "It's just some clothes on the floor—"

"And under the bed, and at the bottom of your closet," Hannah said, pointing to each pile in turn.

"Okay, I admit it—I'm a slob!" Rachel tossed a hanger and a couple of skirts in the air in frustration. "But instead of making fun of me, why don't you help me, you . . . you . . . critic!"

"How?" Hannah wrinkled her nose at the dirty plates littering Rachel's desk and the lipstick smears and kisses on the vanity mirror. Hannah wasn't really up for cleaning anything.

"Write Dylan back for me," Rachel said as she tossed a pink fuzzy slipper and a high heel in the general direction of the closet.

Hannah felt her heart skip a beat. "No," she said firmly.

"Why not?" Rachel asked, grabbing an old Seven-Up can off the desk and tossing it in the trash. "You've done it before. You can do it again."

Hannah had made a secret vow to herself and she wanted to stick to it. "I don't want to do it again. It's your letter, not mine."

Rachel crossed her arms and stared at Hannah for a full minute. Finally she said, "Okay, I'll dictate, and you type."

Hannah frowned. She wasn't sure if that broke her vow or not. The upside was, she wouldn't have to clean Rachel's room. "All right," she said reluctantly. "But make it a short one."

Rachel gave her a quick hug. "Thanks. You're a sweetie." She grabbed the back of Hannah's chair and spun her around to face the screen. Then she began to dictate, "Dear Dylan, I'm five-foot-six, I have thick dark hair and pale blue eyes."

"He knows that," Hannah murmured. "That's why he wrote. He wants to know about you. How you think and feel about things. What makes you tick."

Rachel wasn't listening. She'd crawled back into the closet to finish cleaning it out. Little "Ick! Ick!" shrieks could be heard, punctuated by a flying purse or shoe hurled back into the bedroom.

As Hannah sat in front of the screen, she started thinking about what made *her* tick. Before she knew it, she was typing away.

Dear Dylan,

If I were lounging by a mountain lake watching cougars stalk bighorn sheep, I think my reading choices would be books like *One Hundred Years of Solitude* or *Siddhartha*. Not because they have anything to do with animals (which I love) but because they open doors to other worlds.

I dream of traveling to the usual places: Paris, Rome—and London, of course—but I also long to go to the Serengeti plains of Africa and the

Himalayan mountains in Tibet and
Nepal.

"Ask him if he's going to the football
game this Friday," Rachel called from inside
the closet. "It's School Colors night. I'm
going to wear my gold satin mini and red
angora sweater. It might be cold, though.
Maybe I'll wear my Uggs. Or would that be
too much?"

Hannah only heard the part about the
football game. She was already typing by the
time Rachel began musing about her football fashion ensembles.

This Friday night is the big football
(not to be confused with soccer)
game with our archrivals, the
Spartans from Greeley West. Want to
go? It should be fun. The wearing of
the school colors—red and gold—is
recommended but not a require-
ment.

"Ask him if girls in England wear their
hair long or short." Rachel dragged a black
garbage bag over to the closet and began

stuffing broken hangers, plastic bags from the dry cleaner, smashed shoe boxes, and clothing tags into it. "Oh, and check if he likes heels or flats. I forgot how tall he is."

"Dylan is much taller than I am," Hannah called over her shoulder. "I'd say he's about six-foot-two."

Rachel wiped her arm across her face. "Perfect. I can wear heels."

Hannah rolled her eyes. Sometimes Rachel could be so incredibly superficial.

"Is the e-mail getting too long?" Rachel asked, trying to force a broken hanger into the garbage bag without tearing the plastic sack. "'Cause you can sign off. Just tell him to call me about the game."

"Right," Hannah said, saluting crisply.

> Give me a call if you need a ride to the game. My number is in the student phone book—right next to my e-mail.
>   Ciao!
>   Hannah

Hannah stared at the letter for a moment. She knew something was wrong but she wasn't quite sure what it was. Then it hit her. She'd typed the wrong name! She quickly deleted her name and wrote:

> So long, sweetie!
> Rachel

Hannah hit SEND and promptly slumped in her chair. The fun was over. The soaring feeling she'd had while writing to Dylan had been replaced by a dull tiredness. Because it wasn't her letter. It was Rachel's. Why couldn't she get that into her head?

Early the next morning Hannah was in the middle of brushing her teeth when she heard Rachel's voice calling from outside her window. "Serengeti? I didn't say anything about Serengeti," Rachel yelled. "I don't even know what that is! Is that some kind of pasta?"

Hannah slid the bathroom window open and looked down at her friend, who was standing on the front lawn. In her pink fuzzy bedroom slippers, short plaid boxers, and a white T-shirt that read BABY DOLL, Rachel looked like a character in a sorority girl movie.

"It's a plain in Africa," Hannah said,

taking the toothbrush out of her mouth.

"*You* know that," Rachel said, folding her arms across her chest. "But I don't."

Hannah paused in her brushing. "Your point?"

"My point is, you were supposed to ask Dylan to the football game and find out what he likes in a girlfriend."

"I *did* ask him to the football game, and we already know what he likes in a girlfriend. He likes you." Hannah spit, rinsed out her brush, and stuck it in the water glass by the sink.

"Well, he did say he'd go to the game," Rachel called up to her. "He even promised he'd wear red and gold if I did."

Hannah sighed. "That's great, Rachel. I hope you guys have a good time."

She started to shut her window when Rachel cried, "Wait! You have to come with us."

Hannah's eyes widened in horror. "I've been on double dates with you, Rachel. They rank right up there with visits to the dentist."

"No, no, no!" Rachel hopped up and down like a cheerleader waving her arms.

"This wouldn't be a double date, it would be a . . . a triplet."

"Huh?" Hannah leaned on the windowsill. "Speak English."

Rachel put her hands on her hips. "Do I have to stand in your yard in my PJs shouting up at you? Come on, let me in."

Hannah knew if she let Rachel in, she'd be talked into doing something she really didn't want to do. But she also knew she couldn't leave her outside. Hannah marched down the stairs and threw open the front door. "Look, Rachel, three's a crowd. Everyone knows that."

"This wouldn't be a date," Rachel said, as she hurried through the door. "It would be just a few people going to a game. You could even invite some other friends, like Kyle or Colby."

"But why do I need to be there?" Hannah demanded, as Bongo and Sheila came racing into the living room, howling. Hannah had to shout over their barks. "Dylan likes *you*. He likes *your* looks, he likes writing *you*—"

"Correction. He likes writing *you*," Rachel said, shoving Bongo away from her and patting Sheila, the only well-mannered dog, on the head. "I saw your letter to him. It had nothing to do with me. Here you are writing about that plain in Africa and that other place in Italy, what was it? Nepal?"

"Nepal is not in Italy, Rachel," Hannah cut in. "Naples is. Nepal is in the Himalayan mountains. And so is Tibet. It's called the rooftop of the world. It's where Mount Everest is, and the Dalai Lama, and—"

"See?" Rachel put her hands to her temples. "What if Dylan wants to talk about all that stuff? I need you there to fill me in."

Hannah was torn. The thought of spending time outside of school with Dylan sounded great, even if it meant he'd really be with Rachel. Maybe if other friends were along, it wouldn't be so bad.

"You said he wrote back," Hannah said, gathering up her school books. "What did he say?"

"Here." Rachel reached down and pulled a tight little square of paper from the inside of her slipper. "I brought a printout with me. Read it yourself."

As Hannah took the note she raised a skeptical eyebrow at Rachel's pajamas.

"Aren't you going to school today?"

"Of course," Rachel replied. "I wouldn't miss it. Moynihan is handing back yesterday's algebra test. I want to see his face when he realizes I aced it."

"Interesting outfit," Hannah said, nonchalantly unfolding the note.

Rachel looked down at her sleep shirt and boxers, and a look of panic filled her eyes. "Oh—my—God," she groaned. Rachel turned on her heel and, stepping over Bongo and Sheila, bolted for the door, muttering, "Clothes. Hair. Makeup. Breakfast. No time!"

Hannah would have said good-bye but she was already lost in Dylan's letter.

Dear Rachel,

I've actually been to the Serengeti. In point of fact, to the Ngorongoro Crater. Fantastic! It's absolutely crawling with wildlife. I expected to be overwhelmed by the Big 5: lions, elephants, leopards, rhino, and Cape buffalo. But I was over the moon about the rest of the animals: hilarious warthogs and these amazing huge birds called marabou—they look like vultures in tuxedos—and tiny deer called dik-diks. I have photos that I'd be happy to bore you with.

In the meantime I'd love to see an American football game (and right you are—our football is what you call soccer). And I'll try to be supportive and wear my new school's colours.

See you there.

Dylan

Hannah carefully folded the note and tucked it into her messenger bag. Maybe if she went with a group to the game, it wouldn't be so bad after all. She was dying to see Dylan's pictures of Africa. All she had to do was talk Rachel into asking him to bring them.

When Hannah opened her front door to leave for school, Rachel, wearing a three-tiered black mini and an Andy Warhol punk rock T-shirt, came racing over from across the street. She carried a piece of toast in one hand and her black platform shoes in the other. A Liberty print backpack dangled from her elbow.

"Did you make up your mind?" she asked, getting into the passenger side of Hannah's truck.

"Yup," Hannah said, turning the key in the ignition. "I'll do it."

Rachel put her head on Hannah's shoulder. "Thanks, pal. You're the best!"

7

"First and ten, do it again!" Hannah chanted, pumping her fist in the air.

It was fifteen minutes into the football game between the Red Rocks Eagles and the Greeley West Spartans. The temperature had dropped twenty degrees from the afternoon and there was a distinct chill in the air. Hannah was glad she'd worn her cargo pants and gold wool cardigan. She'd pulled a red wool cap over her long hair. To keep up the school spirit, she'd wrapped a red-and-gold knit scarf around her neck.

On either side of her Colby and Kyle kept up a running commentary on the game.

"That was awesome!" Colby cried, tugging his red-and-gold watch cap over his ears. "Stockwell just blew past that linebacker like he was standing still."

Kyle nodded in agreement. "The Stock's one fast dude."

Dylan and Rachel were sitting in front of Hannah and the guys. Dylan was wearing a navy blue wool jacket and an incredibly long scarf with vertical maroon-and-gold stripes that he'd wrapped around his neck several times. "It's from my old school. Not quite the colors of Red Rocks," he apologized, "but it'll do in a pinch."

Rachel, as promised, had worn her gold satin mini and pointy high heels. Her red sweater had a cowl neck that draped off her shoulder. With her dark, wavy hair pulled into a ponytail on top of her head, she looked very cute—and very cold. In fact, her teeth were chattering so loudly before the game that everyone around her had offered her some article of their clothing.

Kyle loaned her his North Face down jacket and Dylan had given her his fingerless red gloves. Hannah's Pendleton wool blanket was wrapped around Rachel's legs.

"Pump it, Yazinski!" Colby bellowed, as the fullback took a handoff from the quarterback and powered his way down the sideline.

Two blue-and-gold uniformed Spartans finally brought him down but only after he'd made a gain of fifteen yards for another first down. Once again, the crowd leaped to their feet and cheered, "First and ten, let's do it again!"

Dylan, his hands jammed into his jacket pockets for warmth, turned to Hannah and the guys. "I hate to be a dolt," he said. "But could you explain to me once again this 'first and ten' business?"

"It's easy," Rachel said, with a toss of her ponytail. "*First* we get the ball, and then we go *ten* yards."

"Nice try, Rache," Kyle said, "but it's more complicated than that." He leaned closer to Dylan and, pointing toward the field, explained, "You see, once a team has possession of the ball, they're given four downs."

"Downs?" Dylan repeated. "Now I'm completely muddled."

Hannah took her turn at explaining

the game to him. "They're called 'downs' because the play ends when someone is taken down."

"Get out!" Colby gave Hannah a playful shove. "I thought it was called a down because you get a chance to move the ball *down* the field."

Rachel shrugged. "I thought it was because you get four chances to make a touch*down*."

"And if you don't, then they start their count*down*," Hannah concluded. "Got that?"

Dylan stared at her, unblinking. Finally he said, "Next time I ask a question—shoot me."

"It's a deal," Hannah said with a grin.

"Hey, I'm going *down* for some food," Kyle announced. "Anyone want to come?"

Colby stood up. "I'm *down* with that."

While Kyle and Colby high-fived each other for their wittiness, Hannah stuck her head between Rachel and Dylan and whispered loudly. "I'm glad these clowns are leaving. Their jokes can really—"

"—get you *down*!" Rachel and Dylan finished with her.

The three of them burst into laughter. For a moment Hannah thought how glad she was that she'd decided to come to the game. She didn't feel self-conscious or like "three's a crowd" at all.

Once Kyle and Colby were out of sight, Hannah pulled a large grease-stained paper bag out of her canvas tote. "We'd better eat this popcorn before those guys come back. They're like locusts."

Rachel produced a Thermos from her black LeSportsac. "Dylan, take a sip of this," she said, pouring some into the metal cup lid. "It's the only thing I brought that could keep anyone warm."

Dylan took a deep drink of the steaming cider, and sighed with appreciation. "Ahh! 'The silver apples of the moon, the golden apples of the sun!'"

Hannah recognized the quote, and said, "Yeats. He's my favorite."

Dylan cocked his head. "Mine too."

"Yates?" Rachel repeated, as she handed Hannah a Styrofoam cup full of cider. "Is that a band?"

Hannah blew on her drink to cool it. "No, it's a dead poet."

"William Butler Yeats," Dylan explained. "From Ireland."

"Awesome!" Rachel flashed her winning smile. "Now Ireland is a place I'd like to visit."

"After Tibet?" Dylan asked.

Rachel tilted her head, confused. "Excuse me?"

Hannah's whole body twitched. Dylan was referring to the e-mail she'd written for Rachel, but Rachel hadn't picked up on the reference.

"Aw, come on, Rachel," Hannah said, giving her friend a playful poke in the ribs. "You're always talking about wanting to hike the Himalayas and visit Tibet."

"Oh, right!" Rachel said, finally catching on. "It's either there, or go to that place in, um, Africa."

"The Serengeti," Dylan said, nodding.

Rachel snapped her fingers. "That's the one. With all the lions and tigers—"

"Ha-ha!" Hannah laughed extra loudly. "Rachel knows there aren't any tigers in Africa."

"No, but you certainly might run into one in Tibet," Dylan said. "I believe they have Siberian tigers in the Himalayas."

"And *yetis,*" Hannah added mysteriously. "Have to watch out for those."

When Rachel looked confused, Dylan explained, "Abominable snowmen."

Rachel's eyes widened. "They're real?"

Just then the Eagles scored a touchdown and the roar of the crowd drowned out Rachel's question. Hannah breathed a huge sigh of relief. This was getting too close for comfort.

The cheerleaders ran out onto the field and led the pep band in a rousing rendition of the school fight song. Everyone in the bleachers leaped to their feet and sang along. As Dylan chimed in as best he could, Rachel glanced back at Hannah and mimed wiping sweat off her brow.

"What happened?" Kyle shouted, as he and Colby rejoined Dylan and the girls.

"We were in line at the concession stand and missed the whole thing," Colby added. "Bummer."

"Who scored?" Kyle asked.

Dylan looked at Rachel, who looked at Hannah, who shrugged. "I don't know," she confessed.

"You guys," Kyle said, shaking his head in mock disgust as he sat down. "Why do you come if you don't watch the game?"

"Easy does it, mate," Dylan said, with a grin. "They've got their hands full keeping me from making a fool of myself." He pulled off his muffler and, waving it up and down, began to chant, "Ea-gles! Ea-gles!"

Kyle and Colby quickly joined in, stamping their feet on the bleachers. Soon the entire row had joined in. They finally stopped when the whistle blew to signal halftime.

Then Dylan challenged the girls to a popcorn-tossing contest. "Here are the rules," he declared. "You toss a piece of popcorn in the air, and catch it in your mouth. The one with the most catches is the winner, and has to treat the rest of us to a soft drink."

"It's a deal," Rachel giggled. "I'm terrible at this."

Each of them took a handful and then Dylan tossed his first piece of popcorn in the air. With a deft twist of his neck, he caught it in his mouth. "That's one," Dylan declared, crunching loudly.

"I can beat that," Hannah said, tossing

two pieces in the air. She caught them both. "That's two for me."

Rachel tossed hers and it bounced off the tip of her nose, which cracked them up. Randy Jensen and some junior boys five rows up in the bleachers cupped their hands over their mouths and yelled, "Go, Rachel!"

Rachel waved to the boys and playfully hurled a handful of popcorn at them. This set off a popcorn war with the upper bleachers. The air soon became filled with a snowstorm of flying popcorn.

The halftime show featuring Red Rocks' dance team, the Rockettes, began. But Hannah and Dylan continued their fierce popcorn competition, tossing and counting, "Five, six, seven . . ." By the time halftime ended Hannah and Dylan were almost tied.

"You guys," Rachel said, tossing a stray kernel of popcorn their way. "You're going to run out of popcorn."

Rachel was right. There were only six kernels left, and Dylan was just ahead in the count.

"Keep a close eye on him," Hannah warned Rachel as she tossed her last kernel in the air. "Make sure he doesn't cheat."

Hannah had caught her last three tosses but Dylan missed his. Hannah jumped to her feet and danced in place, chanting, "I'm the winner, okay! You're the loser, hey, hey!"

Rachel teased Dylan, "Our Brit lost his groove and the American girl won."

"Ever gracious in defeat, the Brit salutes the winner," Dylan said, snapping off an English army-style salute, with his palm out. Then he pointed at Hannah and added gleefully, "And in accordance with the rules of the game, the Yank known as Hannah will now treat one and all to our soft drink of choice!"

Hannah stopped dancing. "No way!"

"Yes way," Rachel giggled. "The winner has to fly and buy! That was the rule."

Hannah put her hands on her hips and narrowed her eyes at Dylan. "You tricked me!"

Dylan put his hand to his heart and bowed his head. "I'm afraid I did, milady. But a great general knows when to lose the battle to win the war. Please accept my apology." He peeked up at her through a lock of hair that had fallen across his eye. "And bring me a root beer."

Hannah shook a fist at him in pretend

anger. She scooped her red leather change purse from her canvas tote and started down the bleacher steps.

"Hannah, wait up!" Rachel called. "I'll come with you."

Most of the spectators were on their way back to their seats for the start of the second half. The two girls had to fight their way through the throng clogging the steps.

"I feel like a salmon trying to swim upstream," Hannah shouted as she jostled her way through the crowd.

"If I get knocked down and trampled," Rachel shouted, clinging desperately to the back of Hannah's jacket, "get me a diet Sprite, will you?"

"If you get knocked down and trampled," Hannah cried, "you won't need a drink."

"Then make sure I don't fall," Rachel cried, pushing Hannah through the people. "Before we go to the snack bar, stop at the bathrooms, will you?"

Once they were in the aisle leading under the grandstand, Hannah made a sharp right-hand turn and led Rachel into the girls' room. Inside, a few stragglers were standing in line waiting for a stall.

Rachel moved to the mirror and pulled a brush out of her LeSportsac. As she ran it through her hair, she said, "Dylan is so much fun. I had no idea."

Hannah stepped up to the mirror beside Rachel, and smiled at her own reflection as she applied a tiny amount of cherry lip gloss. "He's probably the best-looking guy to ever go to Red Rocks High," she gushed.

"I don't know about that." Rachel traded her brush with Hannah for the lip gloss. "I think Trevor Parks was pretty hot, but he graduated last year."

Hannah waved one hand. "Trevor was handsome and fun, but he wasn't smart like Dylan."

Rachel paused, holding the lipstick tube in midair. "He *is* pretty brainy, isn't he?"

Hannah nodded. "He's awesome."

Rachel looked worried. "I hope he doesn't think I'm a dimwit. I mean, how was I supposed to know that tigers don't live in Africa?"

"Don't worry about it, Rachel. I'm sure he thought you were charming." Hannah ran the brush through her shoulder-length blond hair, then pulled her red wool cap back onto her head. "Besides, I'm here. If you get into trouble, I'll just bail you out."

"That's what I wanted to talk to you about." Rachel leaned toward the mirror and carefully outlined her lips. "You're such a good friend and I'm so lucky you agreed to come with us." She paused and gave Hannah a confident wink. "But I think I can manage from here."

Hannah frowned. "What do you mean?"

"The football game will be over soon." Rachel folded a paper towel and carefully blotted her lips. "Now we're about to begin Part Two of the evening."

"Part Two?" Hannah repeated. She felt utterly clueless. "This evening comes in parts?"

Rachel nudged Hannah with her elbow and giggled, "I'm talking about the one-on-one."

Hannah was staring at herself in the mirror and actually saw the color leave her face. "Oh. I get it."

Luckily Rachel didn't notice the disappointment so plainly visible on Hannah's face. She was too busy rebrushing her hair and checking to make sure the back hem of her satin mini was even.

"I mean, I don't want to be rude or anything." Rachel took Hannah's hand and gave it a squeeze. "You've been so great. I just didn't want you to feel obligated to hang around after the game too."

When Hannah spoke, her lips barely moved. "I don't feel obligated at all," she said. "You guys have fun."

"Oh, we will. I'm sure of it." Rachel wrapped her arms around Hannah's shoulders and gave her a hug. "Thank you so much for helping me. You're the best!"

Hannah followed Rachel to the concession stand, where she bought a root beer and a diet Sprite and put them in a cardboard tray. She carried them back to the bleachers like someone lost in a fog. She'd been having such a good time with Dylan that she'd totally forgotten he was really on a date with Rachel.

When they got back to their seats, Kyle and Colby were standing with Dylan, cheering wildly.

"Where've you guys been?" Kyle asked. "The Eagles have scored two touchdowns in two minutes."

"This is a major blowout in the making!" Colby crowed.

"It's brilliant," Dylan said, accepting his root beer from Hannah. "I've never seen anything quite like this before."

His cheeks were glowing red from the cold and his eyes sparkled. Hannah felt a twinge of longing as once again she noticed how attractive he was.

Suddenly Hannah didn't feel like staying for the rest of the game. She picked up her blanket, which Rachel had dropped at her feet, and shoved it into her canvas tote. Cupping her hands around her mouth, she shouted to Kyle and Colby, "I'm going now."

"What?" Colby had tied his red-and-gold scarf around his head so that the ends dangled in his face. "This is just getting good. Why would you want to leave?"

Hannah shrugged. "I know how it'll end."

Suddenly the crowd was on its feet again as the Eagles' wide receiver caught a pass and broke for the end zone. Hannah stuck her head between Dylan and Rachel, who were cheering the runner on, and announced, "I think I'm going to leave and try to beat the crowds."

Dylan was so intent on the action taking place on the field that he barely heard her say good-bye. "All right, then," he called over his shoulder. "Ciao."

Rachel looped her arm through Dylan's and leaned in closer to him. The last thing Hannah saw was Rachel resting her head against Dylan's shoulder.

If there was ever a moment in her life when Hannah felt like a fifth wheel, this was it.

By eleven o'clock Hannah was in her night-shirt and in bed. She was just turning out her bedside lamp when the phone rang.

This had to be one of her friends. She grabbed the receiver before it could ring again and wake her parents.

"Yes?" she murmured into the phone.

"Hannah, it's me," Rachel whispered.

"Rachel?" Hannah sat up in bed. "Where are you?"

"Home," Rachel replied.

Hannah flicked open the window cur-tain beside her bed. Across the street she could see that a light was on in Rachel's bedroom. "That was fast. What happened to the big date?"

"I'm not sure," Rachel said. "After the game Dylan offered to drive me home."

"On his Vespa?" Hannah asked. "I thought he was nervous about driving on the wrong side of the road."

"He is." Rachel chuckled. "He told me to hold on tight and remind him to keep to the right."

"Where did you guys go?"

"I wanted to go up to Lookout Mountain. You know, it's an awesome place to park."

Hannah didn't know. She'd heard kids at school, especially the guys in the outdoor club, make vague references to Lookout Mountain, calling it 'Makeout Mountain,' but she didn't have any personal experience. "Did you go there?" Hannah held her breath and waited for the answer.

"No," Rachel said flatly. "We didn't go near it."

Hannah let out a sigh of relief. She couldn't help it.

"Dylan wanted to walk around Golden

and talk!" Rachel sounded outraged. "How boring is that?"

Now Hannah was smiling. She fluffed up her pillow and leaned back against the headboard. "It doesn't have to be boring. What did you guys talk about?"

"All that crap you put in the e-mail," Rachel replied. "I had to do some major bluffing about my keen interest in animals and Africa. And I really got into trouble when he wanted to talk about *Siddhartha*. Gimme a break. I can't even spell it."

Hannah laughed out loud.

"It's not funny!" Rachel protested but she was giggling herself. "I mean, when he asked what was my favorite part, all I could think to say was, 'the surprise ending.' Well, of course, he wanted to know what surprised me about it."

Hannah laughed so hard she snorted. Herman Hesse's book was about a young man's quest for inner truth. It was definitely not a mystery with any surprises. "So what did you say surprised you?"

"I can't tell you," Rachel giggled. "It's too stupid."

"Come on," Hannah pleaded. "You've

called me practically in the middle of the night. Now you have to tell me."

"Okay, I told him I was surprised that the book ended. I mean, how ridiculous is that?"

Hannah paused. "In a funny way, that was a pretty thoughtful answer," she said. "After all, the book is all about Buddhism, and how Time is like a river that flows with no beginning or end. He could have thought you gave a totally Zen answer."

"Whatever. I'm just not into those books without plots. I probably should have told him that."

"Why didn't you?" Hannah asked.

"Duh! He thinks I like the book because I wrote him about it in my e-mail, remember?"

It was strange. Only an hour before, Hannah had been feeling pretty sorry for herself. Now she felt almost giddy with relief. There was obviously no real connection between Rachel and Dylan. "So . . . you guys never got to Part Two of the evening?"

"Oh, yeah, we did," Rachel replied. "I finally threw myself at him, just to shut him up."

Hannah's heart sank. "You kissed him?"

"Of course. Dylan's a totally great kisser," Rachel confided. "He's got very soft lips."

Hannah didn't want to hear any more, but Rachel kept chattering away. "We were down by Clear Creek, just off Tenth Street by the kayak park. And we made out for like five minutes. And then Dylan said he'd take me home."

"That's it?" Hannah tried to hide the happiness she was feeling. "That was short."

"Weird, huh?" Rachel said. "Maybe he was tired. Or maybe it was my breath. Did you notice it smelling bad at the game?"

"I didn't get close enough," Hannah replied. "But if it was your breath, he wouldn't have asked you to walk around town talking to him."

"Good point." Rachel sucked in her breath. "Oooh. I just had a terrible thought."

"What?" Hannah looked out her window again. She could see Rachel framed in her window across the street. They faced each other, talking into their phones.

"What if he thought I was boring?" Rachel asked, putting one hand to her head.

"No way," Hannah said, truthfully. "The

heartbreaker of Red Rocks High could never be called boring."

"Oh, Hannah, I am not a heartbreaker." Rachel scooped her hair to the top of her head and struck a pose in her window, with her chin looking over her shoulder. "I'm really just a harmless flirt."

"Flirt, yes," Hannah said, laughing. "As for harmless, that's debatable."

"I'd just hate to have Dylan think I was dull." Rachel dropped her hair back to her shoulders. "He's really interesting. Besides just being British, he seems very different from all the other guys."

Hannah leaned her forehead against the windowpane. "I know. That's what makes him so charming."

Rachel stretched one arm out to the side and yawned. "Well, I'm not going to stress over this. Maybe the Brits are just more relaxed."

Hannah waved one hand at her friend. "Go to sleep, Rachel."

Rachel wiggled her fingers in farewell and disappeared behind her curtains. Hannah stayed at her window, staring at the house across the street. Why *was* their date so short? Could it be Dylan wasn't so crazy about Rachel after all? Hannah flicked off the bedside light and pulled her comforter up under her chin. It was something to dream about.

8

Saturday was usually Hannah's day to sleep in. That morning, however, the phone rang just before eight.

"Hannah?" her mom called from downstairs in the kitchen. "It's for you."

Hannah put her pillow over her head. "Tell Rachel I'm sleeping," she grumbled. "And if she calls me once more, I'll strangle her."

"This isn't Rachel." Her mother was standing at her bedroom door, her hand held over the mouthpiece of the wireless phone. "It's a boy with a charming English accent who just called you 'Hanner.' Should I tell him you'll call back?"

"I'm up!" Hannah shrieked, tossing off

her down comforter and hopping out of bed in one swift move. "I'm up!"

Dylan was already in midsentence by the time she put the phone to her ear. "Forgive me, Hannah, I'm still eight hours ahead on English time," he apologized. "I'll let you catch your beauty sleep and give you a ring later."

"Dylan!" Hannah tried to cut in but he wouldn't stop talking.

"It's the light, really. It wakes me in the morning, first thing. Back in London it would still be dark at this hour—"

"Dylan!"

"I'm a stupid prat, that's all there is to it."

"Dylan, shut up!"

Hannah shouted so loudly that her mother stuck her head back in the room and gave her a sharp look.

She waved her mom away and hurriedly apologized to Dylan for being so rude. "But I'm thoroughly awake and ready to talk," she added. "So if you don't tell me why you've called, then I really will get mad."

Dylan chuckled. "First off, I wanted to thank you for all the fun at the football game, and to tell you I'm sorry I didn't get a chance to say good-bye."

Hannah didn't want to remind him that he *had* said good-bye but had been too distracted by Rachel to remember it. Instead she said, "That's why you called? To say good-bye?"

"Not at all," Dylan laughed. "I was wondering if by chance you might have the morning free. We could go for that horseback ride you talked about, or perhaps a stroll along the Clear Creek greenway around Golden."

A flurry of butterflies began to churn inside Hannah's stomach as it dawned on her that Dylan was asking her out on a date. Sort of. His date with Rachel must have been a bust if he was asking her out today. Well, whatever—Hannah had no intention of going anywhere near Clear Creek, the site of Rachel's attempted make-out session with Dylan!

"Why don't I make a few calls out to the Obstinate J and see if I can borrow a horse?" Hannah suggested. "Then you and I could check out the sights from the saddle. How does that sound?"

"Brilliant!" Dylan said. "I'll drive us out to the stables on my Vespa."

Rachel's description of her late-night ride on Dylan's scooter popped into Hannah's mind. She chuckled to herself at the image of Rachel reminding Dylan to stay to the right.

"Why don't we take my pickup?" Hannah said quickly. "It's easier and I can toss some gear into the back."

They agreed that Hannah would pick up Dylan in an hour, after calling the stables and after calling Dylan back for directions to his house. That put Hannah in full panic mode. She darted around her room like a whirlwind, trying on different riding outfits in between calling the stable and calling Dylan back.

Hannah's room was a third of the size of Rachel's, and its complete opposite. While Rachel had used the walls of her bedroom to take pink to its most extreme, Hannah favored a soft sage green.

The only decorations on her walls were four framed photos that she had taken during visits to Rocky Mountain National Park. Her favorite one was of a stand of golden aspens in the fall, which hung above her bed. On the opposite wall were pictures of a bank of purple and white columbine growing by a waterfall and a pair of fawns grazing in a Rocky Mountain meadow. Finally a shot of a lone golden tamarack tree piercing a dense stand of evergreens hung beside her desk in the corner.

The only other piece of furniture in the room was her dresser, with a mirror hung above it. Tucked into the frame of the mirror were snapshots of Rachel and Hannah over the years, and a picture of Hannah on her horse, Bo Tie.

Hannah pulled a hanger draped with a pair of neatly folded jeans from her closet. "Nobody but nobody hangs up their jeans," Rachel had scolded her last summer. But Hannah liked a crisp pair of jeans. She favored Tommy jeans for riding. She grabbed her favorite green Patagonia T-shirt. It was her lucky shirt. She'd worn it twice in endurance competitions on Bo, and both times they'd won.

When Hannah finally emerged from her room, her mother was waiting for her in the kitchen. A plate of slightly burnt toast and a steaming cup of hot tea sat on the kitchen counter. "You look pretty today," her mother commented.

Hannah looked down at her clothes. "I'm wearing what I wear every day."

"It's not the clothes." Mrs. Briggs cocked her head, first to the right, and then the left. "I think it's the hair. You're wearing it down, which you know I love. And you're wearing makeup."

Hannah could feel the heat rise to her cheeks. She had put on more mascara than usual. Plus, she'd added a little mauve eye shadow and Sugar Kiss lipstick. And yes, usually she wore her hair in a simple pony-tail or French braid to go riding, but today she wanted to look special. Leave it to her mother to notice.

"I'm going riding with this new boy at school," she admitted. "His name is Dylan and he's from London."

Her mother arched her eyebrow about as high as Hannah had ever seen it go. "Dylan?" she repeated. "Didn't I hear a Dylan mentioned last night when you and Rachel were leaving for the football game?"

Hannah winced. "Yes, it's the same guy. Last night I thought he only liked Rachel, but there's a possibility that he may be interested in me. Which I know sounds silly."

Her mother, who had just taken a sip of coffee, set the mug down with a loud *thunk*. "Don't sell yourself short, Hannah," she advised. "Rachel is cute and bubbly, but you're the real beauty. You're also more interesting." Mrs. Briggs smiled and shook her head. "Rachel may well have a head on her shoulders but you'd never know it. All she ever talks about is boys and shopping."

"That's not true." Hannah took a bite of her burnt toast and came to the defense of her friend. "Rachel loves clothes, sure, but so do lots of girls our age. And it's not her fault that all the boys fall in love with her. She's fun."

Her mom scooped up Hannah's empty plate and set it in the dishwasher. "All I'm saying is, don't compare yourself to someone else," she said, wiping off the counter with a dish rag. "You are your own unique person."

Hannah wiped her mouth with a paper napkin. "I just happen to like the same boy as Rachel."

"But you just said he likes you," her mother said.

"I said he *may* like me," Hannah corrected. "Which could be complicated if Rachel really likes him."

Her mother waved one hand. "I doubt that it would bother her. I just saw Bryan Meeker pull up in front of her house fifteen minutes ago, and Rachel skipped out to greet him like he was her long-lost love."

"Really?"

Hannah was relieved to hear it. From the moment Dylan had called that morning, she had a nagging feeling of guilt inside her. She didn't want to seem like she was trying to steal Dylan away from Rachel. But if Rachel was already going out with other boys, maybe it didn't really matter that much.

Hannah wrapped her arm around her mother's shoulder and gave her a big hug. "Thanks for the words of support," she whispered. "I really needed them."

She whistled for Sheila, who dutifully scampered out from the den and started barking. Bongo skittered after Sheila. Grabbing her pack and water bottles, Hannah headed out the front door to her pickup, with Sheila bounding at her heels and Sonny the parrot screeching, "Bongo, get down!"

"Just be yourself, Hannah!" Mrs. Briggs called, scooping the terrier into her arms and standing in the doorway. Sam the cat appeared and rubbed against Mrs. Briggs's legs. "Remember, you're one in a million."

Dylan was already waiting outside his house when Hannah pulled up in her red pickup. In his jeans, diagonal-striped shirt, and Levis denim jacket, from a distance he looked like a typical Western teen.

"Very cool jacket," Hannah called, throwing open the passenger door. "You could almost pass for an American."

"What do you mean, almost?" Dylan protested. "I thought I'd nailed the look."

He hopped into the pickup and once again clouds of dust exploded in the air. This time Hannah didn't sweat it. She spun the red Tacoma truck around and headed out Highway 6 toward the Obstinate J.

"It's your riding boots," she said, pointing to his feet. "American boys wouldn't have thought to wear them. Guys like Colby would still be in flip-flops."

"Or trainers," Dylan added.

Hannah grinned. "Another British give-away. Over here we call them sneakers. Or call them by their brand name, like Nikes or Reeboks."

The rest of the drive out to the stables was spent comparing the different ways the English and Americans described the same things.

"We say a 'tin' of tuna," Dylan pointed out, "whereas you Yanks call it a 'can' of tuna."

Hannah nodded. "And we stand *in* line, and you Brits stand *on* line."

"We say to-m*ah*-toes," Dylan began.

"And we say to-m*ay*-toes," Hannah finished.

By this time they had reached the Obstinate J. As they drove through the gate, Dylan added, "And we ride English, whereas you ride Western."

"Aha!" Hannah held up one finger. "On that one, you're wrong. I've been riding English since I was six."

She pulled the truck to a stop by the horse barn and hopped out. She lowered the ⸍k gate so Sheila could jump down, and pulled a small blue nylon daypack out of the flatbed. It held two water bottles and a plastic bag of trail mix.

"Sherry Hodge is letting you ride Tuxedo today," Hannah said as she led Dylan into the barn. "That gelding needs all the exercise he can get."

"Tuxedo and Bo Tie?" Dylan repeated. "Isn't that a little coincidental?"

"They're both from the Shiloh Stables," Hannah explained as they pulled two saddles off the rack in the tack room. "They shared the same owner, whose daughter happened to be a little nutty about prom when they were born."

"Ah, that's another difference. We don't really have prom in England." Dylan grabbed Tuxedo's bridle off a wooden peg above the saddle rack. "At least, not the way I've heard them described here."

"That's lucky for you." Hannah pulled a curry comb and a brush out of a tray full of them. Then she scooped a handful of apple-oat horse treats out of the plastic bin by the door. "Personally I think the whole thing is a lot of expense and fuss over nothing."

"Don't you like dancing?" Dylan asked,

as they carried their gear down the aisle between the horse stalls. "I quite like it myself. Not in a formal way, but in a club."

"I don't mind dancing," Hannah explained. "I just don't like the part where girls go to the hairdressers and spend zillions of dollars to get their hair sculpted into ridiculous shapes on top of their heads. And the guys spend hundreds of dollars renting a tuxedo that doesn't fit and even more for dinner. It just feels like an incredible waste of money."

"I see your point," Dylan said, with a straight face. "Remind me to ask you to prom when the time rolls around. We'll dine at McDonald's and I'll wear my jeans and trainers."

Even though she knew he was joking, the mention of going to prom with Dylan made the butterflies return to Hannah's stomach. She tried to match his lighthearted tone. "Sorry. But I've got my heart set on dinner at Taco Bell."

"You're on!" Dylan laughed.

Bo Tie greeted Hannah with a loud whinny as they came up to his stall. Tuxedo, the next stall, echoed Bo's hello. Hannah and Dylan set their saddles over a rail and went in to get their horses.

"I think Tuxedo knows he's going to stretch his legs," Dylan said, slipping the halter over Tuxedo's head and leading him out into the aisle. He wrapped the loose end of the halter over the rail near his saddle.

As Hannah got Bo Tie ready to ride, she watched Dylan saddle Tuxedo. She couldn't get over how at ease Dylan was around horses. He knew exactly what procedures to follow. First he brushed Tuxedo's coat and picked any rocks out of his hooves. Then he placed the saddle blanket and saddle on Tux's back and firmly tightened the cinch. He even knew the trick of tickling Tuxedo's tongue to get him to open his mouth wide enough for the bridle.

As they walked their horses outside the barn, Hannah said, "I know this must sound strange, but we hardly ever see any guys out at the stables."

"Really?" Dylan seemed surprised. "Why is that?"

Hannah shrugged. "Maybe it's more of a girl thing. You know, they say all young girls are crazy over horses."

"That's another difference between you Yanks and us, then," Dylan said, putting his foot in the stirrup and swinging into his saddle. "In England everyone is horse crazy. It's in our blood. I mean, every other day you see a photo in the tabloids of Prince William playing polo or the Queen out for a morning ride."

Hannah swung lightly into Bo Tie's saddle and said, "All the same, it's nice to have you along for the ride."

On the word *ride,* Hannah gave Bo a slight nudge with her heels and they set off at a walk up the lane leading out of the stableyard. Sheila trotted along behind them, keeping a safe distance from the horses' hooves.

The lane was lined with slender aspens whose shimmering leaves had already turned a brilliant gold in the cool autumn air. The narrow lane opened onto a broad grassy meadow that stretched away from the Obstinate J Stables.

They walked the horses for ten minutes, giving them a chance to warm up their muscles. Then Hannah signaled Bo again, and soon they were cantering through the tall grass. Dylan let her set the pace but stayed right with Hannah, and Sheila outran them all.

Hannah was in her element. This was her world and she felt completely at home in it. At school she often felt awkward as she tried to play the social games of flirting with the boys and gossiping with the girls. But out here on Bo, with the wind blowing through her hair, she felt beautiful and strong. Hannah could ride these trails blindfolded, and felt confident leading Dylan up into the hills overlooking Golden.

When they reached the crest of Sunset Ridge, she pulled her horse to a stop and let him graze on the wild grass. Dylan trotted up beside her and let Tuxedo join Bo in a quick snack.

"Amazing," he gasped, looking out at the sweeping vista that lay before them. "There's everything out here. Mountains, rivers, forests—"

"Housing developments, two freeways," Hannah joked as she handed him one of the water bottles from her pack. "Not to mention the Denver smog."

"No, seriously," Dylan went on, "there's

a grand scale to everything out West that's so impressive." He stood up in his stirrups and looked intently at a dramatic outcropping of rocks in the distance. "What are those called?"

"The Twins," Hannah replied. "They're about six hundred million years old, and hundreds of feet tall."

"I'd like very much to climb to the top of one," he declared. "Is it very far? Can we ride there?"

"Not today. That's an all-day trail ride," she explained. "We'd have to pack in water for the horses. It's awfully dry out there." Then Hannah added, "But you know, it's a very short car trip."

"Really?" Dylan's face brightened at the thought. "Do you think Rachel would like to go with me?"

His words hit Hannah like a punch in the stomach. "Excuse me?" she said slowly.

The look on her face must have startled Dylan because he backpedaled immediately. "I mean, I was only wondering if, you know, er, that might be the type of outing she'd fancy."

"How should I know?" Hannah replied

stiffly. How could Dylan bring up Rachel, when they were having such a nice time?

"You two *are* best mates, aren't you?" Dylan was clearly confused by her response.

"I suppose," Hannah muttered. "But I have no idea what she thinks would make a fun date." Bo snorted loudly and danced in a nervous circle, sensing Hannah's distress. "All I know is that her idea of fun is very different from mine."

Hannah swung the reins hard to the right and led Bo away from the ridge. She felt so embarrassed, and angry at herself. How could she have been such an idiot? Dylan really liked Rachel after all. She'd been a fool to think it could have been any other way.

Dylan trotted next to her, oddly oblivious to the fact that the whole mood of their ride had changed. "Your friend Rachel is a very confusing girl," he said thoughtfully. "In person she seems to be this very pretty but rather ditzy girl. Her e-mails tell quite a different story. In them she's thoughtful and smart, and truly interested in the world." He shrugged. "I just don't know how those two puzzle pieces fit together."

Hannah resisted the urge to turn and scream, "They don't!" Instead she bit her tongue.

Dylan babbled on about Rachel but Hannah forced herself to keep quiet. Then he said, "I mean, I don't generally go for girls like Rachel, but she's just so smart and beautiful. Not like other girls at all."

Dylan started to ask about Rachel's string of boyfriends, but Hannah cut him off. "Listen, Dylan, I just remembered that I have an appointment this afternoon. So we're going to have to cut this ride short."

The smile on his face faded with disappointment, but he remained cheery and apologetic. "Oh, right. Sorry about prattling on and on about your friend. I got a little sidetracked there. This has really been lovely."

It was difficult, but Hannah kept her voice and manner pleasant and casual. The last thing she wanted was for Dylan to think she might have had a crush on him. Especially now that he had revealed how deeply hung up he was on Rachel.

As soon as the trail opened back onto the meadow, Hannah gave Bo the signal to gallop as fast as he could back to the barn. Running for the barn was a bad habit that horse owners didn't like to encourage. But today Hannah didn't care. She needed to get some of the frustration and resentment she felt out of her system. The full-tilt gallop helped, but it didn't fix everything. The things he said about Rachel had really hurt her, even though it wasn't really his fault. He didn't know Hannah wrote the letters or was ever crushing horribly on him. And it didn't help that Hannah thought this was supposed to be a date.

An hour later Hannah dropped Dylan back at his home. As he got out of the truck he thanked her once again. "It's been simply lovely today. You are a superb tour guide."

"It was nothing, really," Hannah said evenly. "I do this all the time. Glad you could come along."

"It's really a British boy's dream," Dylan added with a mischievous twinkle. "To be out riding the range with a beautiful American cowgirl."

Hannah knew Dylan was just being nice, so she didn't respond. She smiled and waggled her fingers good-bye, and drove away.

That night, as Hannah drifted off to sleep, the phone rang again. It was Rachel.

"Hi, girlfriend!" Rachel chirped. "Three guesses who e-mailed me, and the first two don't count."

"Dylan," Hannah said wearily.

"Yes, and this letter totally explains why our date was so weird last night," Rachel said. "He says it's easier to talk in our letters than in person. He felt like we have two relationships going and it's going to take a while for the in-person one to catch up."

"Like never," Hannah murmured under her breath.

But Rachel hadn't heard her. She had already moved on to the real reason she had called. She needed a favor. Again. "Now he's talking about something called the Twins, and gazillion-year-old rock formations, and he's asking way too many questions."

"So?"

"So I need you to write him back," Rachel said. "You know all about that stuff. You're in AP geology."

Hannah sighed. Then she took a deep

breath and said, "I'm sorry, Rachel, but I can't keep writing your letters for you. It's time for you to deal with Dylan yourself."

"What? Hannah, are you serious? I really need you . . ."

Rachel's voice grew faint as Hannah stretched her arm across the bedside table to hang up the phone.

"Night, Rachel."

Hannah dropped the phone back in its cradle and collapsed back against her pillows. The last twenty-four hours had been way too big of a roller-coaster ride. She felt absolutely drained of emotion.

"Sleep," Hannah mumbled to her cat Maizey, who had joined her on the bed. "I need a week of sleep."

9

The outdoor club had agreed to meet at the climbing wall before school on Wednesday. It was a converted racquetball court just off the main gymnasium. The club had spent several long weekends designing and installing the molded hand-holds and footchips that were fastened all over the walls.

Hannah and the guys usually worked out on the climbing wall several times a week. The early-morning workouts helped them sharpen their bouldering skills. Today everyone's focus was on getting prepped for the Cathedral Rock climb coming up that Friday.

Hannah, who always liked these workouts, was looking forward to this one more than usual. She was hoping that the concentrated effort of tackling the wall would make her forget all about Dylan, and get on with the fun of her last year of high school.

When Hannah ducked through the little half door leading into the climbing court, she got her first surprise of the day. Colby was already strapped into his climbing harness, ready to go. Usually Colby was the club member most likely to sleep late and miss the workout.

"Yo, Hannah," he called. "Will you belay me? I'm thinking I'd like to take a stab at Big Rock Candy Mountain today."

That was surprise number two. Colby generally liked to free climb, which meant never relying on the rope for support or balance. That usually limited him to the less demanding routes on the wall. Now he was asking Hannah to secure his line so he wouldn't fall as he went up the toughest climb they had.

"Okay, Colby." Hannah dropped her pack on the bench by the door and pulled her harness out of her locker. "But what gives?" she asked, as she slipped her legs through the loops and buckled the waist-band. "I've never seen you be the first to arrive anywhere."

"I met a really sweet girl at South Table Mountain yesterday," Colby said, passing one end of the gym's ceiling rope through the hinged metal loop, called a carabiner, at his waist and tying off.

"What's her name?" Hannah took her position at the bottom of the climbing wall and looped the end of the rope dangling from the ceiling under her hips.

"Gretchen Orsow," another voice answered. It was Noah, who had just entered the climbing gym. "And she's a major babe."

"Dude. Hands off Gretchen," Colby said as he reached for the chalk beanbag resting on the floor by his feet. "I saw her first." He chalked up his hands to get a good grip, then glanced at Hannah. "On belay?"

"Belay on!" Hannah held out her brake hand, signaling she was ready for Colby to begin to climb.

Colby nodded. "Climbing." He reached for the first handhold on the wall and began his ascent.

Big Rock Candy Mountain was a boulder problem wall. A climber had to traverse horizontally at one point around a protruding ledge, and navigate an overhang at another. There was even a narrow shaft, called a chimney, where the climber had to scoot his body upward by pressing against the two sides. Colby easily climbed past the horizontal traverse, and then swung out onto the overhang.

Meanwhile Noah got a harness from out of his locker and came and stood next to Hannah. "Hannah, you should have seen this girl. She was awesome," he said. "We all looked like Gumbys next to her."

Without taking her eyes off Colby, Hannah murmured, "She's that good, huh?"

"Better." Colby was breathing hard and had to pause between words. "Gretchen is set to climb a big wall next summer."

Hannah was impressed. There were very few big walls in the country. They usually were very steep and took at least three days to climb. "In Yosemite?" she asked.

Colby nodded, but didn't look back.

"She's planning to climb Half Dome in July," Noah explained. "Her dad works for

Outward Bound and he's leading the climb."

Hannah shook her head. "Awesome."

Noah watched Colby feel with his fingers for a hidden handhold just above the overhang. "Careful, Colby," he warned. "That's a tough move. Maybe you ought to Gaston over to that sloper down to your right."

"Button it, Noah," Colby shot back. He lunged for the hold, snagged it with his fingertips, and pulled himself up and over the ledge.

"Sweet move!" Noah chuckled and whispered to Hannah, "Colby's trying to become a world-class climber overnight. He thinks he's going to really impress Gretchen."

"What do you think?" Hannah whispered back.

Noah watched Colby struggle to traverse the east wall of the climbing gym. "If he can't cut it on plastic," he said, referring to the fake wall they were climbing, "I seriously doubt he can impress on rock."

"I hear you!" Colby sang out as he darted up the last few holds and slapped the ceiling. "Yes!" Then he turned and shouted over his shoulder, "Rappelling!"

Hannah let out the line as Colby rappelled down the side of the wall in big bounces. When his feet touched the floor he automatically said, "Off belay."

"Greetings, fellow gym rats," a new voice called from behind them. Kyle was standing by the tiny door as Dylan came through it. With a broad grin, Kyle announced, "Today's the day we initiate Dylan."

Colby and Noah pumped their fists in the air. "All right!"

Hannah remained cool. She reminded herself that Dylan was just a friend, nothing more. She focused her attention on tying her carabiner onto the climbing rope. When she was ready to climb, she made a general announcement. "I'm going up. Who wants to be on belay?"

Hannah had hoped Noah or Colby would volunteer, but it was Dylan who spoke first. "Count me in," he said. "If you'll give me a sec to get ready."

Hannah waited silently as Dylan slipped the harness Kyle had lent him over his khaki cargo shorts. In spite of herself, Hannah couldn't help noticing how good he looked in his chocolate brown T-shirt with dark green hoodie. She bit her lip in frustration. Why did he always have to be so handsome?

Dylan quickly laced up his climbing shoes, and joined Hannah at the wall. He looped the free end of the rope dangling from the ceiling around his shoulders and hips, and called, "On belay."

Hannah responded with, "Climbing."

Hannah reached for the first set of handholds and scrambled quickly up to the first bucket, which was a large secure hold. She was keenly aware that Dylan was right below her, watching her every move. Her AE shorts were made of a lightweight parachute material that sometimes hiked up higher than she liked. She tried to remember if she'd shaved the backs of her legs. Suddenly Hannah found herself worrying about what underwear she'd put on that morning instead of where she was headed in her climb.

Paul Hume sauntered through the door looking like he'd slept in his clothes from the day before. His GRAVITY HURTS T-shirt was torn and rumpled. He wore flowered surf shorts and flip-flops, and his curly red hair stuck out in all directions. "Dude!"

Paul said, slapping Dylan on the back. "I see you're Hannah's belay slave. Awesome."

"Leave him alone, Paul," Hannah called over her shoulder. "He needs to concentrate."

"I'm just going to boulder it over here on Big Rock Candy," Paul announced to the gym in general as he traded his flip-flops for climbing shoes and headed for the wall Colby had just finished climbing. "You know, work on my technique and power."

"Dude! If you're going to solo on that, don't climb any higher than you'd like to fall," Kyle warned with a chuckle. "You look like you just woke up."

"Hey, no cratering for His Coolness." Paul hopped onto the wall and climbed up quickly to the right. "I'm Spiderman."

As Kyle and Paul continued to exchange quips, Noah and Colby were busy working body moves up the chimney crack.

Hannah was gaining momentum as she easily traversed another ten feet of plastic rock. Then she paused for a moment in stem position, her legs stretched wide apart and pushing out from the holds. "I believe I'm stuck."

"I see the smallest chickenhead about

one meter above your left foot," Dylan advised, pointing to a small lump protruding from the wall.

Hannah stretched her leg up and caught the edge under her climbing shoe. She pushed up and off the edge and that gave her just enough momentum for her to "dyno" across to another large bucket. She took a moment to catch her breath. "Thanks," she called down to Dylan.

"It's easy to sort out from this angle," Dylan replied. "And speaking of sorting out . . . I got the oddest e-mail from Rachel this morning. It was quite different from the others."

Hannah gritted her teeth. Dylan had only been with her for five minutes and already he was talking about Rachel. Again.

"Rachel wrote in this short, jerky fashion with half-finished remarks," Dylan went on. "Almost like some sort of shorthand."

"That's because she can't type," Hannah muttered, stretching to catch hold of another edge and pull herself up.

Dylan pulled in the slack on Hannah's climbing line. "It's really quite odd. I sent her another message, hoping to find out what had happened. And she sent back another reply, as strange as the first. Perhaps she didn't have enough time to compose a proper letter."

"Rachel would rather IM on a cell phone," Hannah said, moving vertically toward the top. "That way she only has to use a few letters."

Dylan didn't seem to have heard her. "We'd exchanged some really nice thoughts a few days ago," he said. "Now she's so abrupt. Do you think she wants me to sod off?"

Something clicked in Hannah's head and before she knew what she was doing, she wrenched herself around and yelled, "You know what, I don't care!"

Her movement was so sudden that she lost her grip and fell. Hannah's climbing training kicked in and she called, "Falling!"

Luckily, Dylan was ready on belay. He was able to stop her fall almost instantly. She dangled in the air for a few seconds, then stuck her hands out and grabbed hold of the wall again.

"Rappelling," she announced, and continued her tirade all the way down to the ground.

"I'm sick of hearing about Rachel!" Hannah punctuated each sentence with an emphatic bounce off the wall. "And those stupid letters. Quit writing and start calling!"

Her feet hit the gym floor and she angrily undid her harness. "You can go on and on talking to Rachel about a walk in an alpine meadow," Hannah fumed. "Or a trek through the Ngorongoro Crater in the Serengeti. Yet you have no idea who she really is."

Hannah faced Dylan with her hands on her hips. "Would you just talk to Rachel," she ordered. "And leave me out of it."

Dylan stood openmouthed with astonishment. Hannah didn't want to wait around for his reply. She quickly grabbed her climbing harness, dropped it in her locker, and stomped out of the climbing gym.

10

Fifteen minutes later Hannah was standing in front of the bank of mirrors in the girls' bathroom. She'd gone in to change out of her shorts and into her jeans. Instead, she'd spent most of the time splashing cold water on her face to calm herself down.

Hannah felt embarrassed that she'd shouted at Dylan. She was humiliated that she'd gotten so upset that she fell. Worst of all, Noah and Kyle and the rest of the guys had witnessed her lose her cool.

Suddenly the bathroom door swung open and banged against the stopper on the green-and-white tiled wall. "There you are! I've been looking for you everywhere."

Hannah raised her head and saw Rachel

reflected in the mirror. They were a study in contrasts: Hannah, red-faced, water dripping, in her sweaty gray T-shirt and shorts; and Rachel, perfectly put together in her layered ruffled mini and hot pink cardigan with fake fur collar. A tiny Hello Kitty bag dangled from Rachel's wrist.

"What do you want?" Hannah asked, reaching for a paper towel to hide her blotchy face. She hoped it wasn't about Dylan and her big outburst. Could Rachel have heard about it from the guys? Or even worse, from Dylan himself?

"I need your help!" Rachel waved a spiral notebook in the air. "You promised to go over the notes for world religions with me before school. Need I remind you that we have a test today?"

Hannah sighed, relieved. "Rachel, I'm sorry. I spaced it completely. I went to outdoor club this morning. And I don't have any outs before world religions, so I can't help you."

Rachel waved one hand. "I know that. I just wanted you to know I have been looking for you for an hour. I finally gave up and studied by myself."

"Great." Hannah tossed the paper towel in the trash and moved for the door. The last thing she wanted to do right then was talk to Rachel.

"Wait, Hannah!" Rachel called after her. "Where are you going?"

"To class?" Hannah pulled open the swinging door.

"We've still got five minutes," Rachel said, checking the gold vintage watch pinned to her cardigan sweater. "And I need to discuss something else."

"Let me guess," Hannah said dully. "Dylan."

"That guy is a puzzle," Rachel said, fluffing her hair in the mirror. "I mean, he writes me this long letter that takes me forever to read. So I write him back a short sweet note, and he acts like I'm telling him to take a hike."

Hannah folded her arms across her chest. "So what do you want me to do about it?"

"Write him." Rachel pulled a yellow Post-it out of her wrist bag. "Here's his e-mail address. Tell him I'd just rather talk than write."

The volcano inside Hannah that had

been smoldering in the climbing gym suddenly erupted like Mount St. Helens. "He's *your* boyfriend, Rachel. *You* write him," she barked. "I won't do it!"

Rachel backed away in surprise. "Geez, you don't need to get so upset."

"I am *not* upset," Hannah said, slamming her fist on the sink. "I told you I was done with letter writing and I meant it."

Rachel cocked her head in confusion. "I thought you liked writing Dylan. You guys have so much in common."

"We're perfect for each other," Hannah sputtered. She ticked off the points on one hand. "He's smart and clever. He likes to travel. He loves horseback riding and hiking and climbing. He likes everything I like." She jabbed her finger at Rachel. "But he likes *you*."

"Oh, Hannah!" Rachel gasped in surprise. "You *like* Dylan. You're mad that he likes me!"

"Of course I like Dylan!" Hannah said. "Who wouldn't? He's perfect! And maybe I am jealous, but that's not what's making me so angry."

"Then what is it?" Rachel asked, knitting her brow in a frown.

"You call me at all hours of the night, just to tell me that Dylan didn't kiss you long enough—"

"I'm just confiding in you," Rachel protested. "Hannah, you're my best friend."

Hannah paced angrily in front of the sinks. "And when you're not calling me about Dylan, Dylan's calling me about you. Meanwhile there are guys lined up, waiting to go out with—"

"You mean Bryan?" Rachel interrupted. "Oh he's nothing, just eye candy."

"See?" Hannah stomped her foot in frustration. "You're boy crazy! I'm upset, and all you can think about is which cute boy is interested in you now. Ooh! That is so, so self-centered."

"Wait a minute." Rachel stepped in front of Hannah and said firmly, "You're making too big a deal out of this. This Dylan thing is just some silly e-mails from a boy I barely know."

"No. It's bigger than that," Hannah shot back. "Rachel, you use me. You want *me* to study for your test. You want *me* to write your letters. You even want *me* to win your boyfriend for you."

Rachel's eyes were suddenly filled with hurt. "Oh Hannah, I had no idea you felt this way," she murmured. "We've always done everything together. I thought you liked being part of my life."

"Your life!" Hannah repeated. She shook her head in frustration. "This may come as a big surprise to you, Rachel Truitt, but I actually have a life of my own."

Rachel stared at Hannah for a long time. Finally she said, "Then why don't you start living it?" and walked out of the bathroom.

Hannah stood there, numb with shock. She stared at the back of the bathroom door and whispered, "What just happened?"

Brring!

"The bell!" Hannah looked at her bedraggled face in the mirror. The school day had just started, and Hannah already felt like she'd reached the end. In fact, she felt so terrible that she decided to go home. Forget world religions. Forget Señor Alvarez docking points for missed days. She just wanted to get out of this school.

Hannah quickly left the bathroom. Putting her head down to avoid making eye contact with anyone in the halls, she marched straight for her locker. She spun the lock, opened the door, and tossed her messenger bag full of schoolbooks inside.

Then a voice behind her asked, "Am I right? Did you write the letters?"

Hannah froze. It was Dylan.

"Hannah, did you hear me?" he repeated. His voice was cold and emotionless. "Did you write the letters?"

Hannah kept her back turned to him. "I helped," she confessed.

"And all of the talk about the Serengeti," Dylan asked, biting off each word. "And mountain streams, and wanting to travel—"

"I wrote it," she admitted, still not turning round.

"And what about *Siddhartha*?"

"That, too." Her voice was barely audible.

"Then you wrote everything."

"No!" Hannah turned and faced Dylan. "Rachel wrote the part about going to the football game. And wearing the school colors. And those last two silly e-mails."

Dylan's face was taut with anger. She could see him clenching and unclenching a little muscle in his jaw as he decided what to say next.

"So . . . the two of you sat at Rachel's computer composing the letters together?" he demanded, like a prosecuting attorney in a courtroom drama.

"Yes." Hannah stared down at the tiled floor.

"God, I feel like a right idiot!" Dylan put both of his hands on the top of his head and spun in an anguished circle. "Here I was, believing those letters were sincere and real. And all this time you were just a pair of bored girls playing a prank on the new boy."

"That's not true," Hannah protested. "We were sincere." She shook her head. "No, I mean I was sincere. Everything I wrote in those e-mails was true. I do want to travel to Africa and Tibet."

Dylan pointed an accusing finger at her. "Then Rachel put you up to this trick?"

"No. I mean, yes." Hannah squeezed her eyes shut and let the words tumble out of her mouth. "It was not a trick. And no one put me up to it. Rachel isn't so . . . deep. She didn't know how to respond to your first e-mail, so she asked me to do it. And I sat down at the computer and I just started writing."

Dylan stared coldly at her.

"I was going to stop, I swear it," Hannah said, holding up her right palm. "But when you wrote back about the mountain meadow, I wanted to write you back myself. But it was too late. You already liked Rachel."

"No wonder she was so different in person," Dylan muttered, shaking his head. "She wasn't the same person. I fell for the letter writer—"

"You fell for the beautiful girl," Hannah cut in. "Admit it."

"Maybe at first." Dylan pursed his lips. "But those letters were what won my heart."

Hannah inhaled sharply at his words. But his look cut her dead.

"Now I find out it was only you," Dylan said, in a disgusted voice, "getting your jollies by humiliating me."

"Um, Dylan," Hannah countered. "Can I point out the humiliation I endured? Here you were, seeing Rachel, and then flirting with me on the side—at the stables, on the trail."

A locker slammed somewhere nearby. All at once Hannah and Dylan realized they weren't alone. The halls were jammed with familiar faces. Dylan glanced over his shoulder and saw Toby Baldwin, giggling with several girlfriends a few lockers away.

"Was everyone in on the letter thing?" Dylan whispered, seemingly oblivious to what Hannah had just said. "Kyle and Noah? The others in the club?"

Hannah shook her head slowly. "They had no idea about the letters," she said. "I mean, they knew you liked Rachel, you told them yourself."

Dylan put his face in his hands. "I can't believe I've been so deceived."

They were both really angry . . . and in pain. Hannah reached out to him. The touch of her hand on his arm made him jerk away as if he'd been stung. Hannah lost her balance and stumbled back into the locker.

Once again Dylan reached out without thinking and caught hold of her waist to steady her. Out of reflex she wrapped her arms around his shoulders. His face was only inches from hers. She looked in his eyes, which were filled with hurt, and watched him search her face, looking for some sign that he could believe her. For one strange moment Hannah thought they might kiss.

Then Dylan murmured, "I wish I'd never come to this country," and let her go.

He was gone. Hannah stood in stunned silence, when someone caught hold of her elbow.

"Hannah Banana, are you all right?"

It was Kyle Martinez. He'd witnessed the entire exchange from his locker across the hall. Just hearing her friend's kind voice, Hannah's chin began to quiver. Her reply came out in one anguished sob. "No."

Kyle didn't say a word. He put his arms around her, and she buried his face in his shoulder and wept.

"Hey, Hannah girl," he murmured. "It's okay."

"I'm sorry, Kyle," she said, in between little hiccuping sobs. "I can't help it."

"Go ahead and cry," he said, patting her on the back.

"I said some awful things to Rachel," Hannah blubbered. "And you heard Dylan. I've blown everything. Big time."

"Hey, take it easy," Kyle soothed. "Rachel's your friend. I'm sure she'll get over it. And Dylan will be cool too."

Hannah shook her head back and forth on his shoulder. "I don't think so."

"You did, however, blow a major lip-lock moment," Kyle cracked, as he gently patted her back to get her to calm down.

"Huh?" Hannah raised her head and wiped at the tears that were streaming down her cheeks.

"The British dude's arms were wrapped around your waist tighter than a Gumby on his first big climb," Kyle said with a half smile. "That was a 'let's get together' moment if I ever saw one."

Hannah put her forehead back on Kyle's shoulder. "Kyle, Dylan hates me. He doesn't want to kiss me."

"Wrong!" Kyle shook his head. "I know guys. He's just confused. He's asking for you to give him a sign."

"Sign?" Hannah repeated, a little too loudly. "What sign?"

"Get straight with him," Kyle advised. "Be honest. Let him know how you really feel about him."

Hannah grimaced. "What if he laughs at me, or acts disgusted?"

"What if he doesn't?" Kyle countered.

"You'll never know if you don't try." He squeezed her shoulder and stepped away from her. "I mean, this is it, Hannah. Senior year. The last year of high school. Don't let it end with any lingering regrets."

Suddenly Hannah thought of Noah, and the feelings she'd had for him in middle school. She'd kept them bottled up inside and nothing had ever happened between the two of them. Rachel had told her to start living her own life. Maybe she was right.

Hannah stood up straight and took a deep breath. "Thanks, Kyle," she said. "You're really great, you know that?"

"Anything for a fellow climber," he replied. Then he looped his pack over his shoulder, and whispered, "Carpe diem, Hannah Banana. Seize the day!"

Hannah pulled the Post-it that Rachel had given her out of her pocket and stared at Dylan's e-mail address. Then she made her decision. She would write Dylan one last letter. But this time it would be from her.

11

Dear Dylan,
This is the truth, the whole truth,
and nothing but the truth. I have had
lots of boy friends, but never a
boyfriend. Not because I don't like
boys, but because I was always waiting for the right boy. And suddenly—
there you were.

Imagine my disappointment
when you fell for my best friend. I'll
admit my first letter to you was for
Rachel, but the second one was for
me. With each letter I wrote, I
eagerly awaited your reply, anxious
to discover your hopes and dreams.

I guess I got more than I bargained for, because I discovered my own hopes and dreams. And they all involved you.

Please accept my apology. I never meant to trick anyone. As you can see, this joke is on me.

Yours,
Hannah

Hannah stared at the words glowing on her computer screen. She'd sent the letter the day before. Still no reply from Dylan.

Now it was the morning of the outdoor club's trip to Cathedral Rock. To her surprise, Hannah felt good. She had followed through on her decision. She had finally told Dylan the truth. The only regret she had at the moment was her confrontation with Rachel. She wished she had apologized for being so harsh with her friend.

Suddenly Bongo started yapping. The terrier was quickly joined by Sheila, which meant that Sonny the parrot would soon be shouting, "Down, Bongo, down. That's enough."

A commotion like that usually signaled the arrival of a visitor. But the doorbell never rang, and soon the dogs quieted down.

"Hannah, you better be up and dressed," Mrs. Briggs called from downstairs in the kitchen. "The bus leaves the school in thirty minutes."

Hannah tugged a pair of rust-colored leg warmers over her jeans, then slipped her feet into her climbing boots. She pulled an Irish fisherman's sweater over her polypropylene T-shirt. She knew from experience how cold it could get on the exposed cliffs.

"I packed you a lunch," her mother said, appearing at the bedroom door with a paper bag in her hand. "And someone slipped this under the front door."

"Oh no," Hannah groaned.

"'Oh no' about the lunch or the note?" Mrs. Briggs asked.

Hannah smiled sheepishly. "Um, both."

She took the lunch sack and stowed it in her climbing pack. After her mother had left the room, she unfolded the note and read it.

It was the world religions test from Wednesday. A large letter *A* had been printed in red ink at the top of the paper. Scribbled along the bottom of the test was a little note, written in blue ink.

Hey babe,
See? I can study on my own! Never meant to use
you. Just like being around you. Thanks for your
help and honest words.
     Your B.F.F. (I hope!),
     Rachel

Hannah flipped open her bedroom curtain and was surprised to see Rachel, in her heart-covered boxers, camisole, and pink Uggs, standing on the front lawn, waiting. When she saw Hannah, Rachel smiled shyly and gave a tentative little wave.

Hannah laughed and waved back. It was hard to stay angry at Rachel.

Rachel held her hand up to her ear like a phone and waggled it, as if to say, *Call me when you get back?*

Hannah nodded and gave Rachel a thumbs-up sign. Rachel breathed a visible sigh of relief and turned to run back into her house.

"T minus fifteen minutes, and counting," Hannah's mom called up from the foot of the stairs.

Hannah quickly pulled her hair into a tortoiseshell clip at her neck, grabbed her pack, and bolted down the stairs.

Bonnie Briggs met her at the bottom with a piece of burnt toast and an apple. "Eat this. Have a wonderful time," she instructed as Hannah stepped over and around two dogs and a cat to get to the front door. "And be safe."

Her mother always got a little more anxious on climbing days. "Don't worry, Mom," Hannah said, waving good-bye. "I won't fall."

Ten minutes later Hannah pulled her pickup into the parking lot. The Red Rocks activities bus was already parked in the circular drive outside the school entrance. Noah stood next to Mr. Tredwell, holding a clipboard and doing their standard supply check. Coils of ropes, a canvas bag full of climbing helmets, and backpacks circled their feet.

Hannah did a quick body count. Paul Hume and Kyle Martinez were standing on the curb, chugging pints of orange juice. Colby, late as usual, was just pedaling up the drive on his mountain bike. Only Dylan was missing. He really had quit the club, after all.

Hannah took a deep breath and murmured, "Maybe it's for the best."

By the time she got to the bus, Noah and

Kyle were tossing the backpacks and climbing gear into the luggage compartments behind the seats. Hannah grabbed the bag of helmets and tossed it in on top.

Mr. Tredwell checked his watch. "Right on schedule. If we leave now, we should reach Cathedral Rock in under two hours."

"You heard what the man said," Noah called to Paul and Colby. "Let's saddle up and ride!"

Kyle Martinez touched Hannah on the arm. "Just checkin' in," he said. "How're you doing?"

Hannah wrinkled her nose. She had to admit not seeing Dylan hurt a little bit. "So-so," she admitted. "But I'll be all right, once we're on the road."

Kyle squeezed her arm in sympathy. "Hang in there, brown eyes."

The outdoor club boarded the bus as the rest of the students at Red Rocks High began arriving for school. Hannah went straight to her favorite place, the long seat along the back of the bus, and stared out the window at the parade of SUVs and pickups pulling into the parking lot.

Paul and Colby already had the bus

windows down and were shouting last-minute comments to some girls who were standing in little groups around the parking circle.

The bus driver closed the side door with a wheeze of brakes. As the bus pulled away from the curb, the girls hopped backward to avoid being sprayed by gravel. They were pulling out of the drive onto the road when Hannah caught sight of a familiar figure turning into the student parking lot on a red-and-white scooter.

Hannah watched Dylan bring the Vespa to a stop by the curb. He removed his helmet and called to Toby Baldwin, who was just getting out of her silver BMW. Hannah craned her neck to see more, but the bus finished its turn onto Golden Avenue South, and Dylan and Toby disappeared from view.

Hannah sank down in her seat. Now Dylan was going after beautiful, sexy Toby. Of course. A surge of indignation welled up inside her. Why was every guy so predictable? She folded her arms across her chest and shut her eyes. "That's it, I'm done. Done with boys forever," she said to herself. Especially ones with a lilting accent, a crooked smile, and emerald green eyes.

All at once the guys on the bus started laughing and cheering. Hannah's eyes popped open. Everyone was crowded on the left side of the bus, pointing and gesturing out the windows. Hannah got up to see what was causing the commotion, and nearly fainted.

It was Dylan, driving like a madman on his scooter on the wrong side of the road. He bent forward over the handlebars, trying to keep up with the bus. All the while he beeped the scooter's horn.

"The guy's insane!" Noah cried. "Tell him to get back in his lane."

"Look," Colby shouted. "He's holding something up in the air."

Dylan pulled a piece of cardboard from the inside of his leather jacket and held it out toward the bus.

"It's a sign!" Kyle declared.

"No kidding, dude," Colby hooted. "But what's it say?"

Hannah read the words out loud. "Stop the bus. I'm an idiot!"

Suddenly the wind ripped the cardboard out of Dylan's hands. The sign flew over the top of his helmet and bounced on the highway behind them.

"He better get into his own lane," Mr. Tredwell declared, jumping to his feet.

"Yo, dude, he's got another sign," Paul announced as Dylan pulled another piece of cardboard out of his jacket. He tried to hold it up again. It flapped in the wind, but the guys were able to read it.

"Hannah! Save me!" Kyle and the others shouted in unison.

Mr. Tredwell had already made his way to the front of the bus. "Pull over, Carl," he told the bus driver. "Before that boy has a head-on with a semi."

The driver hit the brakes and pulled off to the side of the road just as a massive logging truck roared past them from the other direction. Luckily, Dylan had ducked behind the bus and onto the shoulder of the road moments before.

He unfastened his helmet and took it off as he ran down the side of the highway toward the bus. The second the driver opened the doors, Dylan leaped up the steps.

"Pardon me for interrupting your climbing party." Dylan took a second to catch his breath, then stepped into the aisle of the bus beside the driver. He held his helmet under one arm and announced, "But I have an enormous apology to offer to Mr. Hume and Mr. Martinez. And—" He looked around the bus for Colby, then nodded in his direction. "You."

"Us?" Paul and Kyle exchanged confused shrugs. Colby looked bewildered.

Dylan turned to Mr. Tredwell. "You see, sir, about a week or two ago, these lads were expounding at length on the virtues of a certain member of your climbing crew. I believe the term 'hottie' was used to describe her."

Mr. Tredwell turned in his seat to look at Hannah, who felt a surge of pink shoot to her cheeks.

"I, however, did not grasp what they were telling me." Dylan touched his temple and explained, "Apparently I was suffering from a rare form of jet lag. One that causes deafness and temporary blindness."

"Is that so?" Mr. Tredwell said, a tiny smile curving up the edges of his mouth.

"Fortunately I have had a full recovery," Dylan said as he walked down the aisle of the bus. "And now my eyes are wide open."

"And what do you see?" Noah asked.

Dylan stopped and, putting his hand over his heart, faced Hannah. "I see before me a true American beauty."

Hannah's pulse was racing so fast she could barely catch her breath.

"This is a girl who's not afraid to be herself," he said, fixing her with his dark green eyes and walking slowly toward her. "She's strong and athletic. She's smart and a bit sassy." His lips curved in a wry smile as he confided to Paul, "She can certainly get her knickers in a twist, if you give her cause."

"Wooo!" Paul put two fingers to his mouth and whistled.

Colby pounded Dylan on the back and urged him on. "Dude! All right!"

Hannah rose slowly to her feet as Dylan drew closer and closer with each word.

"I love her beat-up, dusty truck. Her well-worn cowboy boots. Her big brown eyes." Dylan paused just long enough to toss Kyle his helmet. "Quite simply, I'm over the moon for the girl."

Dylan took a step toward Hannah and she nearly lost her balance. He caught her around the waist and pulled her close. "We've got to stop meeting like this," he murmured.

Before she could utter one word of reply, Dylan pressed his lips to hers. The guys on the bus burst into enthusiastic cheers and whistles, and stamped their feet in approval. Even Mr. Tredwell and the bus driver applauded. *They are soft,* Hannah thought, remembering what Rachel had said once about Dylan's lips. Then she closed her eyes and all thoughts of Rachel, and the cheering squad on the bus, melted away.

Jahnna N. Malcolm is the pen name for husband-and-wife team Jahnna Beecham and Malcolm Hillgartner. Together, they've written four musicals, two movies, three CD-ROM games, and nearly one hundred books, including the popular series The Jewel Kingdom. They met in the theater and were married on the stage using Marlowe's famous love letter "The Passionate Shepherd to His Love" as their wedding vows.

Make sure to catch
the next Love Letters book:

Message in a Bottle

Quinn yelped, nearly losing her balance. She clung to rocks on top of the wall and looked down where the voice had come from. A boy in a blue-and-white rash guard and surf shorts stood just below, grinning up at her.

"Dash!" Quinn clapped her hand to her chest. "What's the big idea, sneaking up on me?" she said, putting her hands on her hips. But she clearly wasn't angry.

"I'd say you're the one doing the sneaking," Dash said, folding his arms across his chest and leaning casually against the wall.

"I'm not sneaking," Quinn replied,

returning to her post. "I'm spying, remember? On Rose and that loony friend of yours."

"Tanner's with Rose?" Dash raised an eyebrow. "What are they doing?"

"They're shaking hands and—" Quinn squinted to get a better look. "I think they're . . ." She leaned back in surprise. ". . . thumb wrestling?"

"Figures," Dash gasped in mock horror. "The guy has no idea how to treat a girl. I think he needs a lesson from the master," he added, tapping his chest.

Quinn played along with him. "And how do *you* treat a girl?" she asked coyly.

Dash stepped up on the jutting stone and pulled himself easily up beside Quinn. "Well, if I *really* liked her I would want to . . . hold her hand." He slipped his palm under her hand and laced his fingers through hers. "Like this."

The touch of Dash's hand against her skin sent a jolt like an electric shock through her body. Inside, her mind was screaming, *He likes me! He likes me!* But on the outside she fought to keep her cool.

For a moment they just sat there,

smiling at each other. Then Dash shifted his gaze to look at Tanner and Rose. "So, why are we spying on them?"

Quinn bit her lip. This was the perfect moment to tell Dash about finding his message in the bottle, and her plan to have Rose deliver her special reply. But all she could think about was that his hand was holding hers. "I was just curious," she mumbled.

Dash didn't let go of her hand. "Curious about what?"

"Curious to see if you were with him," Quinn admitted, embarrassed. "But you aren't. You're here. With me." She glanced at their entwined fingers. "Holding my hand."

Dash grinned. "It's a nice hand."

Love Letters:
Perfect Strangers

And so Madison's school penpal assignment begins. She's busy running for the school election, and is up against Jeremy – her sworn enemy since forever – but soon Madison finds herself putting aside more and more time to email her anonymous penpal, who calls himself 'Blue'. As the election rapidly heats up, so do the messages, until the two are virtually an item – and they've never even met!

Finally, as Election Day dawns, all is revealed – the winner, the loser, and school's hottest new couple.

ISBN: 1-416-91049-2

Love Letters:

Mixed Messages

Jade has had a crush on Zephyr for as long as she can remember. With his piercing blue eyes and spiky bleached blond hair, Zephyr, the music man, is Wheaton High's leading rocker. For four whole years, Jade has worshiped him from afar, she even started playing the guitar in a vain hope that Zephyr would notice her! Finally, with the end of school just around the corner, her friends persuade her to take action and tell him exactly how she feels by writing him a love letter. So having revealed her undying passion, and that she can't live another day without him, Jade braces herself for the reaction – which never comes! There's been a bit of a mix-up – Zephyr never received the letter! Adam got the letter instead! What a complete disaster and total embarrassment... but then again, maybe not...

ISBN: 1-416-91048-4